KU-242-378

THE NIGHT THAT STARTED IT ALL

BY
ANNA CLEARY

MILLS
BOON

All the characters in this book have no existence outside the imagination of the author, and have no relation whatsoever to anyone bearing the same name or names. They are not even distantly inspired by any individual known or unknown to the author, and all the incidents are pure invention.

All Rights Reserved including the right of reproduction in whole or in part in any form. This edition is published by arrangement with Harlequin Enterprises II BV/S.à.r.l. The text of this publication or any part thereof may not be reproduced or transmitted in any form or by any means, electronic or mechanical, including photocopying, recording, storage in an information retrieval system, or otherwise, without the written permission of the publisher.

This book is sold subject to the condition that it shall not, by way of trade or otherwise, be lent, resold, hired out or otherwise circulated without the prior consent of the publisher in any form of binding or cover other than that in which it is published and without a similar condition including this condition being imposed on the subsequent purchaser.

® and TM are trademarks owned and used by the trademark owner and/or its licensee. Trademarks marked with ® are registered with the United Kingdom Patent Office and/or the Office for Harmonisation in the Internal Market and in other countries.

First published in Great Britain 2013
by Mills & Boon, an imprint of Harlequin (UK) Limited.
Harlequin (UK) Limited, Eton House, 18-24 Paradise Road,
Richmond, Surrey TW9 1SR

© Ann Cleary 2013

ISBN: 978 0 263 89974 0

Harlequin (UK) policy is to use papers that are natural, renewable and recyclable products and made from wood grown in sustainable forests. The logging and manufacturing process conform to the legal environmental regulations of the country of origin.

Printed and bound in Spain
by Blackprint CPI, Barcelona

THE NIGHT THAT
STARTED IT ALL

For lovely Amy Andrews,
a brilliant and versatile author and a wonderful friend.

CHAPTER ONE

Since the break with Manon, his long-time lover, Luc Valentin mostly resisted seduction. Sex risked ever more desire, and desire was a downhill slope to entanglement in a web of female complications. Before a man knew it he could be sucked into an emotional shredder.

So when Luc strolled into D'Avion Sydney and the pretty faces at the front desk lit up like New Year's Eve, their smiles were wasted on the air.

'Luc Valentin,' he said, handing over his card. 'I'm here to see Rémy Chénier.'

The first beguiling face froze. 'Luc—*Valentin*? *The* Luc Valentin? Of...'

'Paris. Head Office. That is correct.' Luc smiled. Rarely had his appearance at one of the company offices sparked such a dramatic effect. 'Rémy, *mademoiselle*?'

The woman's eyes darted sideways towards her fellows. It seemed a strange paralysis had overcome them. 'Er...Rémy isn't here. I'm sorry, Mr Valentin, we haven't seen him for days. He isn't answering his messages. We don't know where he is. We don't know anything. Do we?' she appealed to the others. She consulted her mobile, then scribbled an address. 'You might try here. I'm sure if he's in Mr Chénier will be de-ligh—over*joyed* to see you.'

Luc doubted it. Since his plan was to encourage his cousin

to explain the shortfall in the company accounts then wring his unscrupulous neck, joy was likely to be limited.

There would be a woman involved, Luc guessed, driving across the Harbour Bridge under an impossibly blue sky. With Rémy there was always a woman, though in Luc's thirty-six years never the same one twice.

The address was for a sleek apartment complex on Sydney's northern shore. Luc pressed the buzzer twice before it connected. Then for several tense seconds all he heard was the rustle of white noise.

Prickles arose on his neck.

At last, *enfin*, a voice. It sounded muffled, more than a little croaky, as if its owner had a terrible cold. Or had been weeping.

'Who is it?'

Luc bent to speak into the intercom, which hadn't been designed to accommodate tall guys with long bones. 'Luc Valentin. I am wishing to speak with Rémy Chénier.'

'Oh.' Through the woman's husky fog he could detect a certain relief. 'Are you from his office?'

'You could say I'm from D'Avion, certainly.'

'Well, he's not here. Praise the Lord.' The last was muttered.

Luc drew his brows together. 'But this is his apartment, yes?' The place looked like the sort of residence Rémy would choose. All gloss and sharp edges.

'Used to be. Not that he ever seemed to know it,' she added in an undertone. 'Anyway, he's gone. Don't know where, don't care. Nothin' to do with me. I'm outta here.'

Luc's eye fell on a small pile of carefully stacked possessions inside the glass entrance, among them cooking pots and a frilled and very feminine umbrella.

'Excuse me, *mademoiselle*. Can you tell me when was the last time you saw him?'

'Months ago. Yesterday.'

'*Yesterday*? So he is in Sydney still?'

'I—I hope not. Maybe. I don't *know*. Look... Look,

monsieur…' Luc noticed a slightly mocking inflection in the 'monsieur' '…I'm very busy. I can't keep—'

He jumped in quickly before she cut him off. 'Please, miss. Just one more thing. Has he taken his clothes?'

'Mmm…' There was a pregnant pause. 'Let's just say his clothes took a tumble.'

Luc hesitated, picturing the scene those words conjured. He had an overwhelming desire to see the face that went with the foggy voice. 'Are you Rémy's girlfriend, by some chance? Or—perhaps—the maid?'

There was a long, loaded silence. Then she said, 'Yeah. The maid.'

'*Pardonnez-moi*, miss, but will you allow me to come upstairs and speak with you face to face? There are some ques—'

The intercom disconnected. He waited for the door to unlock. When it didn't he pressed again. Finally after one long, persistent ring, she came back on. 'Look, get lost, will you? You can't come up.'

'But I only wish to—'

'*No.* You *can't.*' There was alarm in her tone. 'Go away or I'll call the police.'

Luc straightened up, frowning. What after all would he expect? Rémy had never been known to leave friends in his wake. Though if she was the maid, why would she be weeping?

She must have a cold.

He noticed a box jammed against the glass. Through its half-open lid he saw it was packed with shoes, some of them a little scruffy. Though certainly feminine in shape and size, these were not the shoes of a femme fatale.

He slid behind the wheel of his hire car, wondering what had happened to his powers of persuasion. In the past he'd have had that door open in a second and the maid eating out of his hand. Of course, in the past he hadn't learned what he knew now.

The gentle sex were deceptive. The *gentle* sex were capable of eviscerating a guy and throwing his entrails to the wolves.

From behind a curtain at an upstairs window Shari Lacey watched the car drive away. Whoever he was, he'd had quite a nice voice. Deep, serious and quiet. Charming even, if she hadn't been over French accents. *So* over them.

She shuddered.

In the next thirty-six hours Luc ran through everything at the D'Avion office with a fine-toothed comb. Every file, every Post-It note. Tested Rémy's team until the PA was sobbing and the execs a whiter shade of grey. He sacked the finance officer on the spot. The guy should have known.

Significant sums had vanished from the accounts, neatly siphoned away, while nothing he uncovered gave Luc a clue as to his cousin's likely whereabouts. With the directors' meeting in Paris looming, Luc felt his time was running out. With grim clarity he saw the moment was close when he must let the law loose on his cousin.

A chill slithered down his spine. Another family scandal. They'd dredge it all up again. His embarrassment. The public ignominy. "The Director, His Mistress, Their Dog and Her Lover" splashed all over the world again in lurid, shaming letters.

He stared grimly through the office window at Sydney Harbour, a treacherous smiling blue in the midday sun. One way or another he had to find the *canaille*. Hunt him down and force him to make reparation.

There was one final resort, of course. Luc sighed. He should have known it would come to this.

The family connection.

Emilie, Rémy's twin, was married to an Australian now, but as far as Luc knew she and Rémy had always been close. Despite not having seen her for a few years, Luc thought of Emi with affection. Though she shared Rémy's gingery curls

and blue eyes, she was as different from her twin as a warm,
happy wren from a vulture.

Trouble was, like all the women in his family she wanted
to know too much.

Eyeliner in hand, Shari leaned closer to the mirror. Dark blue
along right lower lid, continue without breaking across bridge,
now ease onto left lower lid.

She winced. *Careful.* While the swelling had subsided, her
bruise was still tender. Her badge. The perfect parting gift,
really, for a mouse. It brightened up her face. It seemed she
could never have compared to all those exciting women Rémy
had known in France. *And* she was too demanding. Suspicious.
Difficult. Too clever for her own good. Too emotional— Well,
that one was certainly true. Too mouthy. Too jealous. Too un-
forgiving. *Frigide.* A frump. Needy. Victorian…

His complaints had mounted over time. No wonder the poor
guy had been forced to seek so much feminine consolation far
and wide.

She knew in her mind the trick was not to believe the things
he'd said, but to ridicule them. Though in her *heart*…

He'd stopped being sweet some time back, but this recent
encounter had been…a shock. Nothing she'd ever anticipated.
Though she needed to remind herself it could have been far
worse. For a while there she'd thought he might actually force
her into sex.

Hot shame swept through her again. To think something like
this could happen to her. The irony of it, when her girlfriends
had so envied her for her sexy Frenchman. At one time. Before they noticed his roving eye. However tactful they tried to
be around her, Shari knew they'd seen it.

But if any of them found out it had come to this squalid
end—the ones she had left, that was—what would they think
of her? Would they assume he'd been violent all along? Would
they think she'd *tolerated* it?

She wished she wouldn't keep thinking of all those battered wives she'd seen on television shows over the years. All those sad women, too beaten down to defend themselves, believing they deserved their punishment, making excuses for their abusers. Forgiving them, walking the domestic tightrope fearful of saying the wrong thing.

She started breathing fast, getting too emotional again. It was no use getting worked up again. She wasn't those women. She hadn't been too entangled in the relationship to see she had to extricate herself. She'd acted swiftly and decisively, give or take a couple of cruel tweaks of her hair. A twist of her ear. A nipple. Shari Lacey would not be, could never be, downtrodden.

From now on it was all good. She was in her lovely old Paddington again, with every pretty street teeming with the sort of inspirations a children's author needed. She had everything to sing about.

Still, it was amazing how a man's fist had only needed to be slammed in her face the one time to leave her as jumpy as a kitten. Thank heavens she'd already dealt with the estate agents and fixed up the details of her move before Fist Day, or she wasn't sure how she'd have coped.

But she was a rational person. She was safe now. She would get over it. The important thing was to fight fear. Not to turn into an emotional cripple, cringing at the sound of every male voice. She could still enjoy men and indulge in a little flirty chit-chat.

Maybe.

Rémy was *not* typical. Her head knew this. Once again, though, it was her heart that was the trouble.

In fact it was a good thing, a needful thing, that Neil was insisting she come to his party. There'd be loads of men there, all quite as civilised as her lovely brother. It could be her testing ground. From this moment on, serenity was her cloak and her shield.

When her hand grew steady again, she lined both lids with

the darker shade, painted a band of purple shadow beneath her eyes and on the upper lids, then switched to the turquoise brush inside the corners, across the bridge and all the way to her brows.

Standing back to examine her handiwork, she felt a surge of relief. Not only was the bruise undetectable, the stripe across her eyes looked quite atmospheric. It was dramatic, maybe a little over the top, but it suited her. Somehow it made her irises glow a vivid sea-green.

If she hadn't been kicking herself over what a fool she'd been, how needy she must have been to fall for such a cliché, she'd have laughed to think of how poor old Neil and Emilie would freak when she turned up looking like Daryl Hannah in *Bladerunner*.

Though Emilie was no fool. She *had* grown up with Rémy.

That set Shari worrying again, so as an added decoy she drew a frog on her right cheekbone.

Now what to wear to Neil's fortieth? If a woman was forced to go to a party wearing a stripe, it might be best to look gorgeous. A little shopping might be called for. Her smile broke through. With her camouflage in place, the frump could go out.

She'd cried her last tear over the man who couldn't love. Cried and cried till she was empty.

It was time to get back on the horse.

CHAPTER TWO

Luc was made to feel abundantly welcome in Emilie and Neil's pretty harbourside home. Luc, and at least a hundred of their friends. The place was crowded, its family atmosphere so warm it was palpable.

Too warm. A reminder of all that had departed from his world.

And, *quelle surprise*, Emilie was pregnant.

It seemed to Luc everyone was. Everywhere he looked from Paris to Saigon to Sydney women were swollen, their husbands strutting about like smug cockerels. The epidemic had spread across the equator.

He doubted he'd have noticed if he hadn't looked, really looked that day, at the *boulanger* in the Rue Montorgeuil strolling with his pregnant wife, a brawny tender arm around her waist. The guy had been so proud, so cock-a-hoop, so in love with life and the world, Luc had carried the image home with him.

Worst mistake in history.

Apparently, when lovers ran out of things to say to each other, the last remedy to propose was marriage. Manon's response to the suggestion of a child had been as swift as it was ferocious.

'What has happened to you, darling? Do you suddenly want to tie me in chains? I am not the brood mare type. If you want *that*, find another woman.' Her smile hadn't diminished the anger in her lovely eyes.

Once he'd recovered from the shock, he'd realised the enormity of what he'd suggested. The fact that some women did agree to sacrificing their freedom and autonomy to reproduce was nothing short of a miracle.

Inclining his head, he accepted another canapé, wondering how long he would have to wait here in this hothouse of domestic fecundity before Rémy put in an appearance. He was beginning to have his doubts it would even happen. Could his cousin have got wind of his arrival? He'd hardly known himself until the last minute, when he was due to leave Saigon and thought of his pleasant Paris apartment waiting for him.

That empty wasteland. Traces of Manon in every corner.

Otherwise he doubted he would ever have dreamed of travelling so far. But from Saigon a few extra hours' hop to Sydney had had its appeal. Deal with the Rémy problem, enjoy a few days of sunshine, blue seas and skies. Postpone work, Paris, his life. What was not to enjoy?

He should have realised. Wherever he went in the world, *he* was there.

At least Emi hadn't changed. Like the sweetheart she was, every so often she darted back to the corner he was lurking in to ensure he wasn't neglected.

Smiling, she offered him wine, her blue eyes so reminiscent of her twin's. Or would have been if Rémy's had ever possessed any kindness, humanity or the tiniest hint of the existence of a soul.

'So tell me, Luc…is it true? Manon is pregnant?'

A familiar pincer clenched Luc's entrails, though he maintained his smile. 'How would I know? I don't keep up.'

Emilie flushed. *'Pardon, mon cousin.* I don't mean to intrude. I was just so surprised when Tante Marise mentioned it. I wouldn't have thought… Manon never seemed the—the type to want babies.'

No, Luc acknowledged behind his poker face. She hadn't been the type when she was with him. But there were only so many forms of betrayal a man cared to discuss.

He steered Emilie away from the blood-soaked arena of his personal life and onto the subject of burning interest to Head Office.

'Do you see Rémy often?'

Emilie shook her head. '*Mais non*. Not so often since he was engaged.' She smiled fondly. 'He is in love at last. I think he has no need of his sister any more.'

Her hopeful gaze invited Luc to think the best of her beloved brother. Fat chance. The notion of Rémy in love with anyone but himself was about as easy to gulp down as this over-oaked blend.

'Maybe he has gone to the outback to see a client,' Emi said eagerly. 'You know he needs to fly to the clients sometimes.'

Luc frowned. 'Without informing his staff?'

Emilie coloured and cast a glance at her husband, who'd just joined them. 'Well, Rémy's always been—private.'

'Secretive,' Neil put in.

'*Neil*. Don't say *secretive*.' Emilie gave her husband a spousely shove. 'I'm sure he's done nothing wrong. He may just have forgotten to leave a message.'

Reading Neil's suddenly bland face, Luc had the impression Neil didn't share his wife's confidence in her charming brother.

Shari took a moment to nerve herself before pressing Neil and Emilie's bell. She'd stopped wearing the ring weeks ago, of course, but if anyone asked her about it, if they even mentioned Rémy's name, she still wasn't sure how far she could trust herself not to turn into a complete wuss and burst into tears.

Too emotional. Just too emotional.

Emilie opened the door.

'*Enfin*, Shari, after all this time…' She stopped short, looking Shari up and down. 'My God. Is it really you? You look…

incroyable.' Emilie kissed her on both cheeks and dragged her inside. 'I adore it. So sexy and *mystérieuse.*' Emilie thought she was speaking in English, but it often came out sounding like French.

With gratifying awe she examined Shari's transformation. The stripe across her eyes was intriguing enough, Shari supposed, but it was her chiffon dress and new five inch platforms that really had Em reeling.

'Oh-h-h,' the darling woman enthused. 'I am *green*. How can you walk in them? But what have you done to your eyes?' Shari's heart suffered a momentary paralysis, but Emilie continued exclaiming. '*Pretty*, so pretty. Is that frog a tattoo, really?'

Shari eased back out of the direct light. 'You know me. Always faking it.'

Emilie giggled. '*No*, don't say so. Now, where's Rémy?' She peered out into the dark street.

Shari tightened her grip on the strap of her shoulder purse. 'Rémy isn't coming.'

'Not?' Emilie looked nonplussed. 'Oh, but…quick, phone him. Tell him he has to. Our cousin is here to see him and he's looking so stern everyone is terrified.'

Shari looked steadily at her. 'No, Em. I can't.'

Emilie blinked bemusedly at her, and Shari was about to drop the bombshell when more guests piled in through the gate and hailed the hostess.

Shari seized her escape.

'Catch you later.' She smiled, and walked through to the party like a woman riding a storm.

It was a while since she'd visited. As things had deteriorated on the engagement front, she'd chosen to avoid the perceptive gazes of her brother and Em. Little changes had taken place in their home since the last time she'd dropped by to hang and read to their little girls.

Tonight the rooms were crowded, people spilling from the

living rooms to the pool terrace. A small army of hired staff was flitting about, distributing hors d'oeuvres like largesse to the poor.

Heading for a quiet corner, Shari felt conscious of eyes turning to follow her. For a scary moment she feared her stripe wasn't holding up, until a likely lad stepped in her path and told her she looked hot.

Hot? Oh, that glorious word. Pleasure flowed into the dry gulch where her self-esteem had once bubbled like the tranquil waters of an aquifer. Her spine stiffened all by itself. She loved the sweet-talking hound.

Standing way taller on her new platforms, she blew him a kiss. 'Too hot for you, sweetie,' she tossed over her shoulder as she swished by.

There now, that wasn't too hard, was it?

She greeted a few faces she recognised, flashed a wave here, a smile there, just as though everything in her little corner of the world was hunky-dory. She hoped no one inquired about her so-called fiancé. She should never have promised to allow Rémy time to break the news to Em in his own way. She might have known he'd never drum up the courage.

Face it, she'd known all along she should have told Neil and Em herself. Weeks ago, she saw now, instead of feeling she had to avoid them all this time. How much could she tell Emilie about her beloved Rémy, though? It was clear she couldn't reveal anything tonight, with her sister-in-law under pressure.

And she'd have to be careful how much she told Neil. She'd long sensed he didn't like Rémy. He'd always been so protective of her, heaven knew what he might do if he knew about this last thing. And how might that impact on Emilie?

She spotted Neil then, standing in a group with a tall, dark-eyed, sardonic-looking guy who was scanning the room, looking gloomy and detached.

Luc noticed his host waving at someone and suppressed a yawn. These Australians were so open. So forward. So relentlessly friendly and lively. To a jet-lagged Frenchman, a houseful of them was overwhelming. He listened, nodded, made meaningless conversation with strangers and mentally gritted his teeth.

These days, an hour in any roomful of couples was an eternity.

He watched a couple's unconscious linking as they chatted with other people. Hands brushing. Hips. Under duress he could admit to himself he missed those touches. The tiny automatic intimacies a man had with his lover.

At least he lived cleaner now. No promises, no lies. And no pain. It was honest, at least.

As though in ridicule of this absurd reflection a pang of yearning sliced through him. If only he could grow *used* to this life with no alleviating softness in it. No excitement. No warm body to open to him in the deep reaches of the night. What he needed was a…

Through a chink in the crowd his eye was snagged on a flash of colour. He looked. And looked again. He caught a fleeting glimpse of a face, and for a minute the breath was punched from his lungs.

The crowd moved, and now only her soft blonde hair was visible to him. He waited, not breathing, until she angled his way again. Ah. An intriguing sensation thrilled through him. It was her eyes. They were fascinating. So deep and alluring and mysterious. Eyes to haunt a man.

He felt his blood quicken.

The crowd parted again and he was able to take in the whole of her. She'd have fitted in well in any nightclub, but in this assembly she looked almost theatrical. Fragile, with her long legs in the high heels, the soft chiffon dress slipping off one shoulder, neat little shoulder purse knocking against her hip.

Mesmerised, he couldn't drag his gaze away.

Shari smiled as a waiter proffered a tray. She helped herself to a shot of vodka, downed it, then replaced the empty glass and took another to be going on with. She was casting about for a friendly face when she noticed the dark-eyed guy still watching her, his brows lowered and intent.

What the...? Had she broken the vodka laws?

His eyes had a strangely hypnotic quality. A girl had to ask herself if it was really the vodka that was so capturing his attention.

She attempted to crush his impudence with a haughty glare, but he didn't even flinch. Shaken by a momentary pang of insecurity, she hastily drowned it with another gulp of the potato elixir.

For goodness' sake, she was at risk here of tipsiness, not a good thing in platforms. If the guy didn't look away soon she'd be unable to lie on the floor without holding on.

Luc was aware other women were probably present. Pretty women with breasts and soft hair. Women with an air of mystery. Blondes. Legs, long and lovely, shimmering with every slight movement.

He just hadn't until this moment burned to touch one particular one.

Shari eyed her vodka guiltily. Although why should she? She was free, single and twenty-eight, and it was a party. She called the waiter back and rescued another glass from the tray. Turning then to face her examiner, she held them up and waved them at him, then took a sip from each.

His frown intensified. He shook his head at her a little, and she felt her blood stir thrillingly. At the same time a nervous shiver slithered down her spine. This guy was inviting a connection. The question was—what kind?

Shari flicked a glance about to see who else he might be with. He must belong to someone. In that swish dark suit and black silk shirt only a madwoman would have let him out on his own.

But no. At this actual moment, he only seemed to be with Neil.

His dark eyes swept her, bold, sensual while at the same time mildly censorious. Was he disapproving of the vodka, or what? If it had been Rémy he'd have been pouring the stuff down her throat to make her more compliant.

This vodka was a highly underrated substance. She could feel a warm glow coming on. Amazing how it could boost the confidence. Despite the fabled ice packing her mouse veins, she was pretty sure if she passed by that guy she could scorch him with her body heat.

In a roomful of people, why not give it a shot?

Enough of all this shillying and shallying, surely it was time to hug the birthday boy. With a deep breath, and assuming her most glamorous and mysterious expression, she summoned her inner Amazon and swished across to Neil, where she planted some lipstick on his cheek.

'Happy birthday, bro,' she said huskily.

Dear old Neil looked appreciatively at her. 'Didn't I see you in the movies?' He gave her a brotherly hug, then peered into her face. She had to steel herself not to flinch away for fear of him spotting the reason for her disguise. 'That's not a tattoo there, is it?' He wrinkled his brow. 'What do you think, Luc? Do we want our women branded with frogs?'

But the guy's dark velvet gaze had travelled well beyond her frog. He was drinking her all in, razing her to the parquet. True, tonight her curves were exceptionally appealing, but anyone would have thought this was the first time he'd ever laid eyes on a woman.

Though she seriously doubted it. Not with his bones.

Her chiffon top slid off one shoulder and she saw his eyes flicker to the bare section. Against all the odds, a shivery little tingle shot down her spine.

The guy queried Neil without taking his eyes from her. *'Qui est-elle?'*

'My sister,' Neil said, his arm around her. 'This is Shari. Shari, meet Luc. Em's and Rémy's cousin.'

'Oh.' An unpleasant sensation rose in the back of Shari's throat and she took an involuntary backwards step. The door guy. He hadn't mentioned being related.

The guy's eyes—*Luc's*—sharpened, while Neil goggled at her in surprise.

Recovering her party manners with an effort, Shari pulled herself together.

'De*light*ed,' she lied through her teeth. Lucky she was holding the two shot glasses and wasn't required to touch Rémy's cousin. Just her luck though, Neil chose that moment to exercise what he considered his brotherly prerogative, and snatched the glasses from her.

'Thanks for these,' he said, and swilled the contents one after another.

Trapped. There was no preventing the Frenchman from taking her hand.

'Shari,' he said. '*Enchanté, bien sûr.*' He leaned forward and brushed each of her cheeks with his lips.

Oh, damn. Her skin cells shivered and burned, though they'd been inoculated against the male members of this family.

Not that this guy resembled the Chéniers, with their reddish hair and blue eyes. Where Rémy was impulsive, surface cute and brutal, this cousin seemed more measured. Graver. Seasoned. Harsher face, experienced eyes. Dark compelling eyes, with golden gleams that reached into her and made her insides tremble.

'Do you live nearby?'

Ah, the voice. The deep, dark timbre was even more affecting without the intercom, that tinge of velvet accent around the edges.

Clearly he didn't recognise hers. She guessed she must have sounded different over an intercom with a busted eye and a swollen nose.

'Paddington, across the harbour. And you?'

'Paris. Across the world.'

She cast him a wry glance beneath her lashes, and he smiled and shrugged. The tiny, instantaneous communication lit the sort of spark in her blood a recently disengaged woman probably should have had the taste to ignore.

In a perfect world.

No wedding ring marred the tanned smoothness of his hands. A faint chime in her memory struggled to retrieve something of a story she'd once heard over coffee with Emilie. Something about a Parisian cousin, possibly a Luc—or did she say a duke?—and a woman. Some sort of scandal.

If he was the one, she didn't care to imagine too closely what had happened with the woman. His part in it.

'I see stripes are in this season.' He continued to hold her in his gaze. 'Do you always binge on vodka?'

'Unless coke's on offer.'

Beside her, Neil choked on the bruschetta he was wolfing. 'Steady on, girl. Luc'll get the wrong impression.'

She'd forgotten Neil. Smiling, she patted the brotherly shoulder. Neil needn't have worried. Luc was receiving her loud and clear, all right. For one thing, he seemed drawn by her rose carmine lipstick. She was in a likewise hypnotically drawn situation. The more she looked, the more she liked. Her eyes could scarcely unglue themselves.

He didn't seem at all fazed by her coke pun either. Instead, he smiled too, as if he understood she was kidding but it was a secret shared only by them.

'You don't look like a Chénier.' Heavens, was that her voice? Suddenly she was as throaty as a swan.

'I'm not a Chénier,' he said at once, a tad firmly. 'I'm a Valentin.'

That was all to the good. She tried not to betray herself by staring, but his mouth was so intensely stirring she couldn't resist drinking in the lines. Stern, yet so appealingly sensuous. A mouth for intoxicating midnight kisses. The trouble was, a woman could never be sure how a man would turn out beyond midnight.

'Forgive me if I mention it…' He moved a smidgin closer and she caught her breath in the proximity. 'You seem a little tense. Don't you enjoy parties?'

In need of fortification, she snagged a champagne flute from a passing waiter and let her roséd lips form a charming smile. 'I adore them. Don't you?'

'No.'

'Ah. Then I guess that's why you smoulder. I was beginning to think you were a misogynist.' Like his cousin.

She'd once read a novel in which a Frenchman whose honour was being challenged assumed a very Gallic expression. Perhaps that described the expression crossing Luc's handsome face at that very instant.

She could sense Neil's ripple of shock. It gave her a charge of pure enjoyment.

Luc's dark lashes flickered half the way down. 'I like women. Especially provocative ones.'

'How about dull, mousy, dreary ones?'

He cocked a brow at her, then, amused, glanced about. 'I don't see any here.'

'They could be in disguise.'

His dark eyes lit. 'But what dull, mousy, dreary people would ever think of wearing a disguise? Only very exciting, sexy, playful women do that.'

Her spirit lifted with a warm buzz. At last a man was divining her true nature. She *was* exciting, sexy and playful, given the proper inspirational framework. She felt his glance touch her throat and breasts, and the glow intensified. Imagining his smooth fingers tracing that same pathway, she might have begun to emit a few sparks.

She noticed Neil shift restlessly at her side, then mumble something and drift away.

Alone in a crowded room with a sophisticated Frenchman,

another sophisticated Frenchman, Shari felt her feet edge to the precipice. A whisper of suspense tantalised the fine down on her nape. This *might* have been just a bit of aimless flirting, but something in his eyes, something intentional behind his glance, made the breath catch in her throat.

All men weren't like Rémy. Of course they weren't.

The Frenchman gazed meditatively across the room, then back at her. 'What are you trying to drown with all that alcohol?'

'Tears, of course. My broken heart.'

'There are better ways.'

Meeting that dark sensual gaze, she had no doubt of it. The battered old muscle in her chest gave a warning lurch. *Keep it light, Shari.*

She felt his gaze sear her legs and, smiling, inclined her head to follow his glance. 'Oh. Have I snagged a stocking?'

'Not that I can see. Your legs look very smooth.' His mouth was grave. 'Quite tantalising.'

His fingers were long. Imagining how they would feel curved around her thighs triggered an arousing rush of warmth to a highly sensitive region. Ridiculous, she remonstrated with herself. Inappropriate. Here she was, raw on the subject of men, *bruised*, and he was a total stranger. And so close to family. Family connections were such a mistake.

She supposed she was succumbing to flattery. The sad truth was Rémy's endless series of nubile nymphs had messed with her confidence. Her view of herself had altered. While she'd laughed in his face at some of his insults, always delivered with that mocking amusement, a few had penetrated her heart like slivers of glass.

With a momentary pang of panic it struck her she wasn't really ready to get back on the horse. But her rational self intervened. How would she know unless she tried a little canter?

As though alive to the odds she was weighing, Luc's dark eyes met hers, sensual, knowing. 'Are you with someone?'

Her heart skittered several beats. 'No. Are you?'

'No. It's hot in here, do you find? Will we walk outside in the cool air?' Smiling, he took the champagne from her and placed it on a side table. The flash of his white teeth was only outdone by the dazzle in his dark eyes.

She felt a warning pang reverberate through her vitals and mingle with the desirous little pulse awakened there. The guy was smooth. But what would the old Shari have done, just supposing a Frenchman had ever been this suave?

Oh, that was right. The old Shari would have fallen into his hands like a ripe and trusting plum. But having finally achieved exciting, sexy and playful status, was she to just throw it all away?

With dinner about to be served, people were swarming inside. Only a scant few were left out there on the pool terrace. But what was the guy likely to do? Black her eye? Could she allow herself to remain socially paralysed for the rest of her life?

While she was still wrestling with the possibilities, Emilie came fluttering by. 'Oh, Shari. Good, good, you're looking after Luc. *Luc, pardonne-moi, mon cher*. I so want to find out all the family gossip. But as you see, now I am a little *occupée*…Shari can show you…' One of the staff came to murmur something in her ear, and with more profuse apologies Emilie flitted away to deal with her domestic crisis.

That sealed it. Stepping out into the balmy night air, Shari knew she was doing her sisterly duty. Luc was her responsibility. Looking after him was her given work.

He glanced down at her. 'Do you love that moment when you feel suspended on the edge of something?' His dark eyes shimmered with a light that made her insides frizzle and fry.

'On the edge—of what?' The night seemed to gather around her and listen.

'Something—exciting. Perhaps unforgettable.' His eyes caressed her face with a seductive awareness. 'You're not nervous, are you?'

'Yes.' She gazed at him. 'At this moment, I'm quite nervous.'

He looked taken aback, and she hastened to stutter, 'A—a-are you in Sydney long?'

He made a negative gesture. 'Tomorrow I must fly out. I really came tonight in pursuit of my cousin. There are things I need to discuss with him on behalf of D'Avion. But for once in his life Rémy has done something—great.'

'What's that?'

He smiled to himself, then shot her a glance. 'Failed to show.'

Hear hear, she could have cried above her thundering heart. It was reassuring to know he saw through Rémy. Maybe he was one of her kind, after all.

They reached the end of the pool terrace and paused. Beyond, pale garden lights reflected the moonlight and illuminated the pathway that snaked down through the shrubbery to the boathouse. Beyond, lights glimmered from craft moored in the bay.

She noticed Luc's glance stray towards the path.

With a surge of adrenaline she knew wickedness beckoned down that shadowy track. Or—maybe just friendliness. A respectful cousinly chat. She was no longer engaged. Why should every move be such a struggle?

Though this *might* be the moment she should let slip her knowledge on the subject of Rémy. Tell Luc his charming cousin was bound to be in LA by now. No doubt with a woman along, maybe even the twenty-year-old he'd recently taken up with. That was if he'd been able to find his missing passport, after turning over the apartment *and* her in his fruitless, vindictive search.

It was all so ugly. The old revulsion threatened, and she turned impatiently away from all things Rémy. Tonight she needed to wipe him from her mind.

'Are you very important in D'Avion?' she said conversation-ally, just as if she hadn't noticed their feet were on the path.

The air was heavy with the sweet sultry fragrance of night jasmine. The back of Luc's hand touched hers and her skin cells shivered in welcome.

They turned the corner and were out of sight of the house. Excitement infected her veins with a languor, as if her very limbs had joined the conspiracy.

'Very,' he said gravely, though his eyes smiled. 'And you? Are you in the theatre, by some chance?' She shook her head, and he considered her, his lashes heavy and sensual, his eyes appreciative. 'Let me guess.' He touched her nape, drew a ca-ressing finger down to the edge of her top. Magic radiated through her skin and into her bloodstream. 'Something cre-ative. You give the impression of not always being bound by the ordinary rules. Would that be true?'

Her heart lurched. It was such a line, but all at once it seemed quite possibly true. Especially now she was in disguise.

'Oh, well.' She hated to exaggerate her minuscule claims. 'I guess I'm an artist of sorts.' She flashed him a brilliant smile. Gouache, crayons and cuddly possums didn't go with five-inch heels and red toenails, but they had their excitements.

'So you paint?'

She barely hesitated before she nodded. 'Partly.'

'What does that mean?'

'Well, I write stories for children. And paint—you know, the illustrations. I'm not that good yet, but I have actually had a book published. It's a picture story book about a cat.'

She pulled herself up, not wanting to babble on about her-self and bore the man to tears, but he was gazing intently at her as if genuinely interested.

He drew in a breath. '*Tiens*. Shari, that's very impressive.' He spoke so warmly she couldn't doubt his sincerity. 'You are a genuine author.'

Inwardly, she absolutely glowed. 'Oh, in a very small way.'

He took her hand and pulled her to face him. It had been so long since a man had touched her in that special way. She trembled inside her bones with a nervous yearning. What if she froze and couldn't summon the necessary fire? What if she embarrassed herself and shied away at the crucial moment like a scared animal?

She felt her mouth dry to an uncomfortable clumsiness.

'You are modest.' He said rather hoarsely, 'I think you are not what I expected.'

She said breathlessly, 'What did you expect?' Compelled to moisten her lips, she saw a hot flare in his eyes.

He kissed her then, a firm, purposeful sexy pressure that shot a delicious flame through her blood and made her entire being tremble with longing.

Ready to swoon, she moved against his hard body, opening up to the full sexy onslaught, but he pulled back and released her. He gazed at her, his eyes unreadable, then traced the outline of her face with his finger. He pressed her lower lip with his thumb and her insides melted in the blaze.

'You taste *douce*.' His voice was a little gravelly.

Douce. *Douce*? Was that all? To her parched senses he tasted like man and sex and long, hot nights.

With her adrenaline pumping like crazy, they resumed walking until they reached the end of the path where the boathouse gazed out over the water, its windows blank and enigmatic. As they stepped onto the boardwalk near the landing stage, the moonlight contoured the Frenchman's face with hard lines and angles. She caught the desire glowing in his velvet eyes, and felt confused.

Having seduced her thus far, was he having second thoughts?

'What sort of things inspire you to write?' he said.

'Oh, well.' She made an expansive motion with her hand. 'All sorts. Owls. The moon.' His mouth was so achingly close. Her lips, her entire being hungered to be touched, stroked, enjoyed, caressed, pampered, kissed, *loved*...

Would he touch her again, or was that *it*?

'Owls?' He sounded surprised.

'Oh, owls are really very magical, ethereal beings. Have you…have you ever read—*Rebecca*?'

He frowned in thought. 'What is that? Is it to do with owls?'

'No, no.' She laughed heartily. 'It's…I guess it's a romance. A—mystery. A bit of a thriller. Rebecca has the family boat-house furnished like a private apartment. Her secret love nest where she can meet her illicit lover.'

He lifted his hands. 'I don't think I know it. *Romances, enfin…*' He made an amused, negative shrug.

What an idiot she was. Of course men didn't read romances. Just as well, or they'd know too much.

His eyes glinting, he cast a smiling glance at Neil and Em's boathouse. 'What do you think? Would this one—have furniture?'

All the fine hairs stood up on her spine and shivered in suspenseful, gleeful exultation. She hesitated a breathless instant, then spread her hands. 'Well, we could always see. I know where they keep the key.'

He looked keenly at her. Said offhandedly, like a guy who didn't care one way or the other, 'Are you sure?'

The thing was, though, his voice had deepened in timbre just that betraying bit.

She gazed fleetingly into his eyes, not needing to read beyond that hot, lustful gleam. He cared all right. He wanted her, and she felt propelled by a wicked, reckless desire to mount that untamed stallion and do something wild.

'Sure I'm sure.' Her breath came faster.

She slipped her hand under the iron tile between the pylon and the floor where she'd seen Neil hide the key a dozen times.

Bingo. It was there.

Her hands shook so badly as she fitted it into the lock, she had to hunch to prevent Luc from seeing.

Once inside, she was assailed with the boat smell of paint

and varnish and salty, fishy weekends. Neil's cruiser floated silently in the lower room, a ghostly presence in the silent dark. A flight of steps led to the upper loft where supplies were stored.

Shards of moonlight illuminated the walls. Shari indicated the way, stumbling once on the stairs. Luc took her arm to steady her.

She didn't speak, just turned her breathless gaze to him. Even in the dim light his eyes were burning. Her blood ran hot in her breasts, fanned fire between her legs.

They finished the climb to the loft. She was trembling again, in the grip of something more elemental now than mere nerves. She faced him, aflame.

He pulled her to him. This kiss was a rough and hungry collision, his tongue in her mouth, possessive, lustful, his hands in her hair, moulding her shoulders, unfastening her bra. She dragged at his shirt and fumbled to release the buttons, avid to feel his naked skin beneath her palms.

With the mingled scents of aftershave, wine and man rising giddily in her head, she thrilled as he stroked her breasts. Then his mouth closed over her nipple and the blaze in her blood roared. She sobbed in deep quivering breaths as he slipped his hand inside her pants, caressing, stroking her engorged sex until she swooned with ecstasy.

Then he slid a finger inside her and massaged, sending waves of erotic pleasure thrilling through her burning flesh. She rocked against his hand, maddened, desperate.

'Oh,' she groaned, clinging to his shoulders. 'Yes, yes, yes.'

To her intense disappointment his hand paused. She felt his hot breath on her neck.

'I don't have any protection with me,' he said hoarsely. 'Do you have anything?'

'What? *What*?' She could hardly believe her ears, but the exigency of the moment must have jerked her memory, because she dredged up an image of a thin emergency package in the deepest reach of her purse.

Maybe fate or the devil were on her side, for, scrabbling among the debris, her fingers located the precious article. She held up the battered package.

'Here,' she breathed in triumph.

She saw his eyes as he snatched it from her. Their focused, hungry gleam incited such an intense and burning heat in her, such an inferno of responsive lust, she could barely wait for him to sheathe himself.

Swiftly it was done.

She clung to him and locked her legs around his waist. Then he thrust his virile length inside her again and again, filling her up, stroking the inner walls of her yearning, burning flesh. It was good, so, thrillingly, shudderingly good.

As she felt his fabulous hardness inside her her passion escalated out of control and she zoomed to an extreme and explosive climax. Her first during the actual act. Fantastically, *his* tumultuous spill happened almost at the same time, groans of release shuddering through his big frame while pleasure rayed through her bloodstream like light.

He held her close to his beating heart, crushing her damp breasts, his hot breath fanning her ear. She felt shattered, and bathed in jubilation. She needed to pinch herself. So *this* was what all the shouting was about.

Of course she couldn't rely on it happening every time. It might even have been a fluke, brought on by the forbidden aspects of the scene.

Even so, it was such a precious moment. For a wild minute she adored Luc Valentin. Felt pretty sure she would adore him *and* this boathouse for the rest of her life.

'We should go back,' she breathed into his ear at last. 'We don't want to be missed.'

He held her away from him, his dark gaze urgent, compelling. 'Come with me to the hotel. We'll have a little supper and enjoy each other properly. You will come?' He gazed at her, then kissed her. '*Bien sûr* you will.'

Excited, relieved, she hardly knew what she said. '*Oh*. Well…who can resist a little supper? I'll have to say goodnight to Neil and Em, though, you know. Otherwise they'll wonder…'

His mouth was grave, though his eyes gleamed. 'No, we don't want them to wonder.'

CHAPTER THREE

SHARI slipped from the downstairs bathroom, anticipation bubbling in her veins. Luc was across the hall, waiting. Like her, he was spruced again, as immaculate as if their stolen encounter had never happened.

She started towards him just as Emilie emerged from the dining room. They both halted, Luc backing into a convenient doorway before he was noticed.

'Oh, *chérie*,' Emilie exclaimed. 'I've been wanting to ask you. What's happening with Rémy? Where is he?'

Shari hesitated and glanced past her to see if Luc had heard. Her heart lurched when she saw his expression. He was staring at her, his eyes sharply alert.

'Well, he...I—I—I don't know for certain.' In a low voice Shari added, 'He's gone away, I think. I'll tell you about it tomorrow, I promise.'

But Emilie wasn't to be fobbed off. 'You don't *know*? Come on, Shari, something is going on. We haven't seen either of you for months. He's your *fiancé*. You should know. What game is he playing with you, *chérie*?'

As she felt the blistering intensity of Luc's concentrated gaze on her face Shari's guilty cheeks burned. 'Tomorrow, Em. I'll tell you everything. I promise.'

Emilie looked as if she was about to insist, but some other people burst into the hall, laughing, from the dining room, and she compressed her lips. She threw up her hands and exclaimed in a lowered voice, 'It's always something with him. When will he ever—? *D'accord*, Shari. Tomorrow. Don't forget. I won't sleep until I know.' She hurried away to her guests.

Luc waited until they were alone, then bore down upon Shari, his eyes glittering danger. She felt an involuntary pang of alarm.

Resisting an impulse to back against the wall, she stood her ground. 'I know what you must be thinking,' she said in a hurried murmur. 'It's not how it looks. I can explain.'

'Of course you can.' His voice was smooth as silk and laced with sarcasm. 'You are engaged to my cousin.' His eyes were hard and accusatory. 'That was you in his apartment.'

'Shh,' she whispered, glancing towards the nearby dining room. 'Yes, yes, it was me, but *no*, I'm not his fiancée. Not any more. The engagement, such as it was, has been broken for weeks. Months.'

'Then how is it Emilie doesn't know? Your sister-in-law?' He looked incredulous.

'Well…I—put off telling them. Rémy's her brother, Neil's *my* brother…' She spread her hands. 'Em has had difficulties with her pregnancy and… She's so attached to Rémy, and any bad news is bad for her blood pressure. Rémy talked me into keeping quiet because he wanted to break the news himself.' She grimaced. 'He's probably dead scared of some of the things I might tell them.'

'What things?' His dark eyes were stern.

She glanced at him, then darted a glance towards the living room. 'This isn't a good place to talk. I'll explain more when we're alone.' She slipped her hand into her purse and grabbed her mobile. 'Do you have your own wheels, or shall I phone for a cab?'

'A moment.' He raked her with his eyes, then turned sharply away from her as if the very sight were deadly. He crooked an elbow over his eyes, shading them from some dangerous glow she emitted. His voice sounded as if it were being wrenched

from the centre of the earth. 'This—*break-up.* Just how recent is it?'

'I *said.* I *told* you…' Her voice faltered a little. She could see
where he might be headed with this. 'Not that recent.'

'*How* recent?'

She started to feel annoyed at his tendency to fire questions
like bullets. 'Well, officially I gave the ring back a couple of
months ago. Though by then it was well and truly on the rocks.'

'"*Officially*".' He made mock quotation marks with his fingers. There was a definite snap in his voice that riled her. 'What
does that mean?'

She glared at him. 'Look,' she whispered fiercely, 'not that
it's anyone's *business*, but he and I imploded almost at the start,
only like a fool I kept on…'

He swung about to impale her with his gaze. 'Forget the
excuses. Give me a straight answer. When was the last time
you were together?'

Her blood pressure rose. 'Does that matter?'

'It may not to some guys, but I have a strong distaste for
screwing women who are still hot from my cousin's bed.'

She flushed. 'I'm not *hot from his bed.*' Her chest heaving
with indignation, she added sweetly, 'Though until a minute
ago you could have said I was hot from your arms.'

For an instant his eyes flared, then he concealed them behind his dark lashes. 'When was the last time you saw him?'

'Wednesday, okay?'

'This week?' His frown intensified, though his glance
strayed to her mouth.

'Yes. He was looking for his passport. He accused me of
holding onto it after I threw his things out of the apartment. As
if I would. He said he had to go to LA on the firm's business.'

A tinge of contempt touched his face. '*Vraiment.* So…did
you give him the passport?'

'I told you. I didn't have it.'

His dark eyes flickered over her, searching, suspicious. It

was pretty clear he didn't believe a word she said. The hackles rose on her neck. She was so *over* being insulted by the men in this family.

'So,' he said with maddening silkiness. 'You sleep with a man on Wednesday, then you sleep with his cousin on Saturday.'

She hissed in a long, simmering breath. 'Only if his cousin's very, very lucky.'

The raw anger in her voice finally penetrated Luc's brain. She wasn't taking his perfectly natural concerns well. As he scanned her face his certainties suffered a jolt. There was a sparkle in her eyes that gave him pause.

Her luscious mouth was firmly compressed, when only minutes ago those lips had been so soft and yielding, so tinglingly responsive.

She turned away from him.

With quicksilver rapidity a dozen arguments flashed through his mind. From her point of view she might have been telling the truth. She was a woman, after all. What woman ever understood the dictates of honour between men? Particularly men of the same family?

The night's original agenda scintillated in his mind's eye. Perhaps he was being harsh. Overly fastidious. If she was no longer *officially* engaged...

And he'd be gone from Australia tomorrow. They'd be ships in the night, et cetera. Passing on the stormy seas of his bed at the Seasons. Plunging and plunging in the sweet, fresh sheets, her naked beauty his to enjoy to the full. Totally naked, and by lamplight...

Gazing at her sweet profile, he felt a renewed urgent stir in his loins. It would be too cruel to have to sacrifice this now. Rémy would never have to know.

At that admittedly seedy reflection shame started to seep through him. What was he doing? He'd come to relieve Rémy of his job, not his woman. For all he knew they'd had a mere lovers' tiff and she'd be back in his bed in a few days.

Avoiding looking at her for fear of succumbing to temptation and throwing honour out of the window, he chilled his tone. 'Let's be adult about this. I think we have to acknowledge that our recent—interlude—was an error of judgement.'

She turned coolly on her heel and stalked away in the direction of the front door.

'*Shari.*' Galvanised to action, he caught up with her in a couple of strides.

A mere beat ahead of him, she was first to grab the door knob. As he reached over her blonde head to take it from her he heard a small startled sound issue from her throat and just for an instant he noted a curious rigidity in her. He touched her shoulder and she started, then spun around, alarm in her eyes.

'*Pardonne-moi.*' He drew back in concern. 'I didn't mean to scare you.'

'You *don't* scare me. And you'd better believe that.'

Bemused by the tense glitter in her eyes, he tried to placate her. 'You're upset. Shari, please.' He gestured imploringly. 'Be reasonable. Maybe you're angry with Rémy. Try to understand, I cannot allow myself to be exploited as a weapon of revenge in some—dispute between lovers.'

'*Exploited,*' she echoed, her voice low and trembling. '*Revenge.*' She closed her eyes. 'Oh, why didn't I see? You're just like him.'

'How am I like him?' he retorted, stung.

Her eyes sparkled fiercely. 'Everything you're saying, every word is—is—accusing me of *cheating.* You're calling me a-a-a slut.'

His blood pressure made a surprising leap, but he cooled that purely visceral response. 'No,' he said coolly. 'I am far too polite.'

She wrenched the door open and walked quickly down the path.

After a second, driven by some impulse, he strode in pursuit. He'd almost caught up to where she stood outside on the pavement, when without warning she dashed forward and hailed a passing taxi.

The car drew into the kerb and she scrambled in. As it moved into the road she turned to cast him a last icy, burning look through the window.

He felt stunned. *Nom de Dieu.* What sort of guy did she think she was dealing with? With fire flaring in his veins, he raced for his hire car.

Attempting to keep her cab in sight among the many, he wove in and out of the traffic—absurdly heavy for a country of this size—rationalising his impulse. At least if he talked to her again he could explain his position more fully. Surely it was important to leave their encounter on a positive note.

They were practically family, weren't they? She'd be grateful, as he would be. After all, it had been a fantastic few minutes they'd shared. Fantastic.

Her silky softness still seemed to be in his senses, her voice, her very *essence*… His hands tightened on the wheel. If he was honest, he wasn't ready yet to call it quits with her.

They left the Harbour Bridge behind, wound a way through the neon city and plunged into a maze of narrow one-way streets lined with terraces. Having lost the taxi a couple of times, he *thought* he still had the same one in view, and was heartened when he saw the name Paddington on a shop front.

Wasn't that where she'd said she lived?

Just his luck, he was trapped on the wrong side of a red light. By the time he started again, the cab was out of sight.

He cursed long and colourfully. Taking the direction he calculated his quarry must have taken, he crossed a couple of intersections before he reached one where he caught a fleeting glimpse of someone alighting from a stationary cab. The distance was too far for him to be certain it was Shari, but it was a chance. His only chance.

Curbing his impatience, he recircuited the block and waited for the lights again, drumming his fingers on the wheel in his urgency to backtrack.

By the time he reached the terrace he'd estimated was the one, the cab was well and truly gone, the street quiet.

Breathing fast, her heart still thumping painfully, Shari paused in the delicate task of stripping her face bare. She would not accept the verdict. She wasn't guilty of anything.

She'd done nothing to feel ashamed of. She didn't care what Luc Valentin thought of her. She'd allowed him to enjoy her body purely out of generosity.

She took some deep calming breaths to slow herself down, then, when her hand was steadier, gingerly dabbed the paint from the bruise, revealing it in all its violent glory.

Was it her imagination it looked worse? She cleaned her teeth, then changed into her flowery old oversized tee shirt and slipped into bed. Lying there in the dark, she rolled the events of the evening around in her mind.

It was *his* problem if he couldn't appreciate an honest human exchange without labelling a woman. And the insulting way he'd refused to believe a word she'd said. What was that all about?

She was startled from her reflections by noise from outside. Her heart thudded until she remembered tonight was the neighbourhood's bin collection night. Hers was crammed full to overflowing with trash left by the previous tenants.

She should get up and take out the bin. She should.

From his park across the street Luc scrutinised the row of houses in the terrace. He suspected 217 could be the one, for a light had recently gone out in its upper front window. Now the entire house was in darkness, as was its neighbour.

What if he was mistaken? He began to see how ridiculous his mad chase was. He couldn't knock on every door in the terrace. And how likely was Shari to open the door to him anyway? She'd probably accuse him of stalking her.

Le bon Dieu, he *was* stalking. Whatever it was about her that had got under his skin was compelling him to linger there even now, when he knew he'd lost any opportunity he might have had if only he'd been able to keep the cab closer.

It wasn't as if he could throw pebbles at her window. The chances were he might terrify some poor little old lady to death.

He was about to cut his losses and call it a night when he heard a familiar rumbling, then at 221 an old guy came into view hauling a wheelie bin. He trundled it through his gate and parked it next to some others lined up under a streetlight.

A minute or two later one after another all the lights came on at 219.

Luc waited, watching, then his heart leaped. Another bin was being wheeled from the gate of 219, this time by a woman.

A *blonde* woman.

He got out of the car and strode swiftly across the street.

She'd changed from her party clothes into some long, flowing robe-like garment, but as he drew nearer he saw it was Shari. Admittedly, his heart was beating a tad too fast for a cool guy in charge of the situation.

She angled the bin into line with its neighbours just as he caught up with her.

'Shari.'

She jumped, and with a strangled cry started back through her gate.

Realising the enormity of having suddenly seemed to appear out of the dark, he was filled with contrition. 'Shari.' He only just restrained himself from grabbing her. 'Forgive me for startling you. I—I only want to talk. I just want to explain...'

'Luc.' Her voice was stunned, incredulous. 'Do you have any *idea*...? What—what are you even *doing* here?'

He noticed her draw the lapels of her garment close and

fold her arms across her breasts. It affected him with a burning desire to hold her to him, kiss her hair.

'Shari,' he said thickly, advancing on her. 'Shari...'

The light fell full on her face then, and he narrowed his eyes for a closer look. With a gut-wrenching shock he saw it wasn't a shadow darkening the area surrounding her right eye.

She turned sharply away, covering the bruise with her hand, and started striding for the house. 'Leave me alone.'

After a second of stunned paralysis, comprehension flooded through him and he was aware of a sharp twist in his chest. Her whimsical make-up had had a purpose, after all. He bounded after her onto her little verandah with the blind intention of pinning her down and making her talk to him, but she reached her door first.

Before she could close it, he rammed his knee against it. 'What happened? Who did that to you? Was it him? Rémy?'

'Of *course* not. What do you think, that as well as being a slut I'm a...a...? I had an accident, all right?' She was flushed and trembling, so achingly vulnerable in her fierce pride he felt something inside him give.

Accident, *vraiment*. He couldn't believe that. At the fragile pretence he felt so torn with tenderness and remorse, he hardly knew what he was saying, only that his voice grew hoarse. 'Shari, *chérie*. Don't be so...I didn't mean to imply... This— this is *not* how we should say *au'voir*.'

In the verandah light her naked face was strained, her eyes dark with emotion. 'We are strangers. We will never meet again. Move away from the door, please.'

She closed it in his face.

CHAPTER FOUR

But the world as Shari knew it jolted off its axis. It was Rémy she never saw again.

Soon after dawn one morning in the autumn, Neil came hammering on her door with the shattering news. Rémy had been driving too fast on a foggy Colorado mountain road, misjudged a corner, and skidded over a cliff.

The shock was so immense, Shari was overcome with nausea and had to run to the bathroom to throw up. The details were sketchy, but it was clear Rémy hadn't been alone in the car.

What a surprise.

In the hours that followed, once Shari had begun to assimilate the news, she wished she could cry. At least poor Emilie had that release. Em was so distraught, so overcome with grief, Neil was beside himself with anxiety for her health and that of their soon-to-be-born twins.

The best Shari could do was to change into her old track pants and run for miles, thanking heaven Luc Valentin wasn't there to see her in her running clothes. Her emotions were a mess, not improved by an even more than usually massive dose of PMT.

She tried not to speculate about what Luc would be thinking about Rémy's loss, and concentrated on feeling sad. Of course she must be, deep down. She must be torn with sadness, though the main feeling she was aware of was her sympathy for Em.

Overcome as she was, as they *all* were, she refused to delude herself about Rémy.

His death didn't change the cruel things he'd done. Some of the wounds he'd inflicted had had a bitter afterlife.

All right, maybe her plunge into adventure with Luc had been a bit soon after the end of the engagement, but officially—*technically*—despite the things Luc had said to her, she had done nothing wrong. Impulsive maybe, to share pleasure with a man who couldn't appreciate a woman's generosity in the best spirit, but not wrong.

She'd stick to that even as Luc Valentin tied her to the stake and applied the flaming torch.

No. If she did feel any guilt, the real reason, the one she could never admit to Em, was that, where Rémy was concerned, the worst she could feel was this terrible, awful hollowness. On the other hand, where Luc was concerned, she felt—

Raw.

The shock shook some Parisian quarters as well. In his executive office high above the Place de l'Ellipse, Luc Valentin was riveted to the police report, his pulse quickening by the second.

The loss of a young life was a tragedy, of course, though his cousin hadn't exactly endeared himself to many of his relatives. Luc guessed poor Emilie would be the one who suffered most. The only surprise was that it had been an accident. Despite Rémy's oily ability to slip out of tight situations, the chances had always been that eventually someone would murder him.

Someone like himself.

He'd considered it a few times after his tumultuous encounter in Sydney.

All at once finding his office suffocating, he took the lift down to the ground.

He strode block after block, seeing nothing of the busy pavements as the vision that haunted his nights invaded his being.

Shari Lacey, powerful, vivid, as searing as a flame. Shari, her emerald eyes glowing with the sincerity of her denials. Shari…

Her very name was a sigh that plucked at his heartstrings. No, he mused wryly, wrenched them. If only Australia hadn't been so far away. If he could talk to her. Hear her voice…

In the midnight hours he'd once or twice considered taking a month's vacation and taking the long flight back. Just to— catch up. See if she needed protecting.

Those last bitter moments at her house stayed with him. *We are strangers* still rang in his ears. In English the words sounded even harsher than they did in French. That cold click of her locking her door, locking him *out*, had reverberated through him with a chill familiarity.

He grimaced at himself. Suddenly women were rejecting him on both sides of the world. Why? He'd never been a guy to pursue an unwilling woman. *Vraiment*, until Manon's sudden betrayal he doubted he'd ever before experienced one. All his life, he'd taken for granted his ease at acquiring any woman he desired.

But first Manon, and now Shari… Somewhere on the journey, he'd lost his way.

Maybe he should have stayed in Australia and persevered. If it hadn't been for that crucial directors' meeting he might have stayed and… What?

Remonstrated with her? Sweet-talked her? Tried to make her *forget* Rémy? But how could he have? What man would dream of trying to impose his will on a woman who was already wearing the evidence of brute masculine force?

His fists, his entire being clenched whenever he thought of it. If he ever came across the *canaille* who'd done that to her…

He felt certain it had been Rémy. No wonder she'd been weeping when he'd gone to the apartment in search of him. How could such a woman have been sucked in by the guy?

He threw up his hands in bafflement.

Was that why Shari had insisted her wound had been an accident? She was still in love with her fiancé, *ex*-fiancé, whatever he'd been?

One thing was certain, whatever her status that night, she wasn't engaged now.

Nom de Dieu. This impulse to contact a woman on the other side of the world, make some sort of approach, remind her he was alive, was ludicrous.

His feet slowed at the place where the red-curtained windows of a bar spilled an inviting glow into the grey afternoon.

Signalling the bartender for cognac, he took a table by the window. A couple of women came in and sat down. One of them had fair hair, not unlike Shari's.

He drew the accident report from his pocket and re-examined it. Had they told Shari about the other woman in the car? Maybe she was in despair, grieving for the *coquin*.

He took out his mobile, calculated the time in Australia, then with a gesture of impatience slid the phone back into his pocket.

A blonde woman at the other table turned his way.

He dropped his glance, conscious of disappointment. There wasn't the slightest resemblance.

Jolted from sleep, Shari dragged her eyelids apart as her phone vibrated with maddening persistence. She stretched out her hand for the bedside table.

'Hello,' she croaked.

'Shari. *Ça va?*'

The masculine voice slammed Shari with a sickening shock. Her heart froze.

'*Rémy?*'

There was a nightmare instant of suspense, then the voice, contrite, apologetic, said, 'Shari, *c'est moi*. Luc. I'm sorry if I'm disturbing you.'

'Sorry? You're *sorry*?' The relief, the warm, weakening relief flooded through her like a sob and gave her back her speech. 'Do you *know* what time it is? Phoning in the middle of the night and speaking French… Are you trying to *terrify* me? And d-d-did you think I would want to speak to you ever again in my life? How did you get this number, anyway?'

'From Neil.' His voice dried. 'Forgive me. I see this was a mistake.'

'*Another* mis—' she started to say, but Luc Valentin, the man who felt disdain for her, the man who knew her shame, disconnected before she could finish.

She lay awake until dawn, staring into the dark, alternately regretting her anger, then burning with it all over again. If only he hadn't surprised her that night without her make-up. If only he'd left her some shred of dignity, she might not have had to feel so angry with him. She might have been able to hear his voice without all this agony.

It seemed her agony was never-ending. The excruciating reports of the efforts to reclaim Rémy went on for days before he was recovered. Messages flew thick and fast between Sydney and Paris. Luc's name came up so often in Neil's conversation, Shari wanted to cover her ears.

It was hard enough trying to squash down her memories of the party night. Shari didn't *care* if Neil thought Luc was a great guy. But she couldn't say so. She just had to grin and bear it all. And of course, poor Emilie needed to reminisce and talk about Rémy and her other family members. The least Shari could do for her grieving sister-in-law was to listen.

Emilie produced some photos of a visit she and Neil had made to France as newly-weds, before Rémy emigrated. One in particular smote Shari's eye. It was of a foursome, leaning against a ramshackle fence in some rural setting. Rémy and Emi were linking arms with Luc and a spectacular-looking brunette with cheekbones and long, straight, shampoo-model's hair.

'See, Shari? Here's Luc and Manon. This was the day we visited Tante Laraine's farm. Do you remember, Neil? How happy we all were?' Her eyes filled with tears.

'Oh, Em.' Shari put her arms around her and stroked Em's hair. Naturally, anyone in tears always brought hers on as well.

When they'd all mopped up, Shari glanced again at the picture, once or twice. Manon was beautiful, no doubt about it. Some would say she and Luc looked good together. *Right* together, both being so tall and good-looking. Though Shari was not one of those people. How people looked was hardly the point.

She tried to persuade herself Luc didn't appear all that happy in the picture. He wasn't exactly grinning like the others, just smiling a little at Manon in that amused sort of way that made his eyes warm.

It scraped her heart. She turned away from it. Family photos had never interested her, anyway.

As it happened, she knew enough about Manon, since naturally, after the Luc debacle, she'd come across a few things on the Internet about Manon and her sensational affair with Jackson Kerr. Not that she was all that interested in Kerr and Manon at Cannes, or Kerr and Manon in LA. There'd been a million articles about Kerr's discarded actress wife, with the usual wild gossip over the trashing of the marriage.

The tabloids had been pumped with it all when the affair was fresh, though now after all this time it had gone off the boil.

Luc hardly came in for a mention, except she saw his name mentioned in a couple of French newspaper articles about business. Who cared, anyway?

She buried herself in work. Anything to blot out reality.

She was involved in mapping out paintings one morning for her owl story when a magnificent bouquet of flowers was delivered to her door. Wow. It must have been ruinously expensive. Carrying the fragrant mass in to join her accumulating hothouse, she opened the card.

And felt a rapid pounding in her temples.

To Shari. Sincere condolences for your tragic loss from my heart. Luc Valentin.

She sat at her kitchen table, staring at the card, smarting. What did he mean by it? He knew enough about Rémy. He'd seen her bruise. Was he using this occasion to needle her?

Meantime, Neil continued to pour information into her unwilling ears. While Rémy had recently made his home in Australia, he'd still kept his French citizenship. His true heart had always been in Paris, according to the family. He must be transported there and buried in the family tomb.

'Emilie's devastated that she can't go, Shari,' Neil's voice issued down the phone. 'Not with the twins so close.'

'Oh, of *course.* I know. It's such a shame.' Shari felt so sad for poor Emilie, and helpless. 'Poor Em. It's a horrible tragedy. But what can she do?'

'She thinks someone must go in her place.' Neil's voice faltered a little. 'We er...we know you'll want to be there, Shari. So we're—counting on you.'

Shari blenched to the soles of her feet. *'What*?'

The image of Luc Valentin, backed by a phalanx of hostile aunts, turned her hoarse. 'Neil, *no.* Rémy and I didn't even part as *friends.* Far from it. He wouldn't— *They* wouldn't want me there. I don't even know Paris. I—I—I...*Neil.* You know I can't afford it.'

'Don't worry, lovie,' Neil said with surprising gentleness for a brother who was usually fairly brisk. 'We'll buy your ticket. We insist. It's the least we can do for you.'

'But... *Please,* Neil, tell Em I'd love to represent her, but I can't. You of all people know I'm no good with funerals. And I'm too... Lately I've just been so tired. And I haven't a thing to wear. Anyway, I hardly know a word of French. Neil, Neil— I couldn't bear that long flight.'

There was a long silence. Then Neil's voice came through again. Serious this time. Kindly. 'Sis... Listen to yourself. You *need* to do this. Em and I have seen how down you've been these past weeks. You're not yourself.'

'What do you mean?' Though she knew as soon as she said it she'd probably been tetchy and miserable. How could she have been anything else? Rémy had *died*, for goodness' sake. She'd never been able to handle death.

As well, she'd been shamed by a man she'd offered herself to, she was struggling to create a book, and if all that weren't bad enough her PMT crisis had gone on for so long her boobs were exploding out of her bras.

'Emilie and I have talked it over. You're in denial, we think.'

'Neil.' She laughed hollowly. 'Don't be silly.'

Typical of her brother to come up with some pop psychology. If only it were possible to explain to a man without him immediately leaping onto the bandwagon of sexist propaganda about hormones affecting women's intelligence.

The truth was, stress had always given her menstrual problems, right back to her high-school days. Crushes, exams, falling in passionate love with her English teacher... The pangs of adolescence had thrown her querulous body clock out of whack every time.

She knew from experience that once her period started, she'd feel better in every way and be able to cope properly and be a decent, loving support to her sister-in-law.

'Come on, Shar. The truth is you've been grieving over Rémy and the engagement a long, long time. We think you need to make this pilgrimage to properly close this episode in your life.'

Oh, *right*. Where did they get their psychiatric expertise from? Doctor Phil?

A few retorts jostled on her tongue, but most of them would only add fuel to Neil's assertion that she wasn't being herself. Her mousy, frumpy, slutty, hormonal self.

'We absolutely *insist* on sending you first class,' Neil persisted, enthusiastic since it didn't have to be him. 'See? You can sleep all the way. It'll be a rest. And don't worry about Paris. The family will look after you. Look how well you got on with Luc.'

Visions of the boathouse, their hot, panting urgency, Luc's hard length filling her up, making her cry out, making her *wild*, making her yearn *every night since*, sent Shari's knees weak. 'No,' she said faintly. 'You're wrong about that. We detested each other.'

'Are you sure? It hardly seems like a week since you were here fluttering your lashes at him.'

Shari wanted to shout *Stop*. If only he knew what he was saying. Every word was a spike in her heart. Considering that Luc Valentin was the only person now living who knew the shame of her battered woman status...

Considering she'd actually had *sex* with him...

Considering he thought her the lowest, most pathetic creature he'd ever laid his aristocratic eyes on...

And how recently she'd snarled at him on the phone like a wild animal.

She shuddered to the core. She could never face him again.

'Come on, Shar. *Please*. If not for yourself, do it for Emilie. Em wants to ask you herself, but she's afraid you'll think she's imposing on your generous nature.'

Right. Fine. The Big One. The Emilie card.

Emilie was fragile, Neil reminded her. The twins could be distressed. Any further disturbance could bring on a premature birth situation. They could *lose the twins*. They could lose Emilie.

Shari's conscience twinged. She loved Em as much as she loved Neil. With sinking resignation it dawned on her she didn't have a chance of wriggling out of it unless she wanted to feel shame and self-reproach for all time.

Succumbing to the intense and excruciating pressure by painful degrees over days, she accepted that this was what family members did for each other. For once in her life she must put aside her personal fears and phobias and do something for someone else. Regardless of what Luc Valentin thought, she did have courage *and* self-respect, and she could behave honourably, and like an adult.

She could go there and meet him on his home turf with cool composure.

Though she did lay down some stipulations. She would only go briefly. And she would arrange it all herself. She wanted no interference.

There would be no advance warnings given. She made Neil solemnly promise on his honour as a brother and a stockbroker. No jolly welcoming committee at the airport. No feather bed tucked under the charming rafters of Tante Laraine's rustic roof.

Emilie was shocked and wounded at this—Tante Laraine was her mother's beloved cousin, *and* the mother of Luc—but Shari insisted. She would rather stay in a hotel.

She would rather stay in a drain.

All right, she could admit to herself she was scared. Call her a coward, but everyone knew the French loathed strangers. Especially if they couldn't speak the language creditably. Rémy had always found her attempts to use her high school French hilarious.

Naturally, the last thing she wanted was to stay in a household where her name was a byword. One of her deepest fears was that Luc would have informed his entire family about the whore of Babylon Rémy had engaged himself to. It wasn't as if she'd be able to defend herself there by telling them the truth about their golden boy.

Boys.

And as if everything else weren't enough, the truth was, as Neil very well knew, she'd been severely traumatised by funerals ever since her mother's. If Neil hadn't been there to put his arms around her quivering ten-year-old self in the bad days and nights that had followed she'd probably have had to be sectioned.

Dragging herself to the task, she booked a room in a hotel near the Louvre. At least it didn't sound too bad. There was something solid about an Hôtel du Louvre. If her nerve failed her when it came time to attend the ceremony, she could always sneak to the museum and hide among the Egyptian antiquities.

The flight she booked was transferable, just in case anything came up where she was required to stay longer. If Luc Valentin got over his disgust at the way she'd spoken to him on the phone, he might feel forced to take her to dinner, or something. She should probably accept, for the family's sake, although she'd be reserved, even rather chilling.

She took steps to ensure she had something decent to wear to the ceremony. Luc might have a low opinion of her morals and her self-regard, but she would give him no opportunity to sneer at her clothes. Rémy had often declared that a Frenchmen could only ever feel distaste for the woman who was careless of projecting her beauty.

It had never been any use explaining to him how easy it was for an author/artist to forget to change out of her pyjamas for twenty-four hours when in the grip of her muse. Even Emilie had wrinkled her nose when she found out her guilty secret. Shari doubted Luc would be any different.

Just as well she wouldn't be there long enough to get found out. She would establish a lasting impression of herself there as a woman of faultless grace and dignity.

Taking Emilie's advice, Shari stuffed the corners of her suitcase with scarves. A woman could get away with much in Paris, Em promised, so long as she wore a scarf. Along with the scarves Shari included a massive pack of tampons. When her period finally, blessedly, did eventuate, it was bound to be Niagara Falls.

The moment arrived when, braced for every kind of horror, she boarded the flight.

By the time she disembarked at Charles de Gaulle mid-evening twenty-five hours later, among other things she was feeling rather wan. An hour before landing, a minor bout of turbulence had made her lose her dinner. Fear, no doubt, combined with motion sickness.

She cleaned herself up as best she could, scrubbed her teeth and sponged her neck, but her hair was lank, her clothes wrinkled and her breasts felt tender and vulnerable.

At least no unwelcome man loomed up in Arrivals to witness her failure to project her beauty at the airport. One thing she never wanted to give Luc Valentin the chance to see was Shari Lacey in transit. He'd seen more than enough.

Soon she was in a taxi being whisked incognito through the streets of the City of Light.

Though it was officially spring, Luc's home turf must have been suffering a cold snap. A drizzly rain obscured its fabled beauty and chilled Shari to her soul. When she alighted from the cab, her teeth chattered.

She glanced around her, pursing her lips. So this was Paris.

Drawing her thin trench coat around her, she regarded the hotel with grim misgiving. Its façade was imposing, in keeping with the surrounding palaces on the grand boulevards.

But a smiling porter strolled out to take her bag and usher her through the revolving doors, and inside, thank the Lord, the lobby was warm, the people surprisingly welcoming.

Feeling empty after her mishap during the flight, Shari planned to order a snack from the restaurant. But once settled in her airy room with its long, graceful drapes at the windows, all she had energy for was the hot shower she'd craved the last five thousand miles. Then, clean, warm and comforted, she slipped between the sheets.

CHAPTER FIVE

SHARI woke to the pale grey light of a Paris dawn. Straight away the horrors of the day ahead sprang into her mind and her stomach swam in total rejection.

Naturally. There wasn't a lot to look forward to.

Rémy, in his c—*situation*. Luc Valentin on his home turf. Remembering his last view of her. Judging her. Looking the way he looked in her dreams. So damned sexy.

She dressed with gentle movements so as not to antagonise her insides. It struck her that every garment she donned was doubly appropriate. Funereal, for mourning, and sinful, sultry and black for her wicked, whorish nature.

Emilie had lent her a beautiful, elegant silk suit from her pre-pregnant days. Shari had to suck in her breath to close the skirt zip, but at least the cinched-in waist flattered her curves, especially her breasts in the new lacy C-cup she'd bought to accommodate the recent rise in volume.

With sheer black stockings and high heels, she judged the overall effect satisfactorily black, and possibly more elegant than she'd ever achieved to date. Now for the hat.

She'd managed to prevail on Em for a loan of her wide black organza Melbourne Cup number with the luxuriant velvet rose adorning its brim. Shari loved the gorgeous thing. All it lacked was a veil.

Positioning it carefully over the simple chignon she'd managed to achieve, she had the wistful sense it still made something of a disguise. None of her friends would have recognised her. Perhaps Luc wouldn't.

Though she'd smoothed on some make-up, her strain shone through. Staring at herself in the mirror, she understood breakfast wasn't even a remote possibility. Lucky for her the bar-fridge offered a convenient bottle of the blessed black fizz, among other things. She crammed it into her shoulder bag for later. Just in case.

All too soon the dreaded moment came. With a dry mouth, Shari took the lift down and asked the concierge to find her a taxi. The guy obliged by strolling out to the kerb and summoning one with a piercing whistle. Normally that would have delighted an Aussie girl from Paddo. Not today.

Shivering, she climbed into the taxi like a serving wench into a tumbril. Neil and Emilie had provided her with all the details she needed. Rémy, her former lover, fiancé and abuser, was to be buried at Père Lachaise.

With her feet pressing an imaginary brake through the floor, Shari was carried inexorably through the cemetery gates. The car followed a winding street through a city of stone. At the very end loomed a domed chapel.

Her heart lurched. Gathered in front was a small congregation of mourners, all garbed in black. But superimposed on her vision of all of them was Luc. He was standing a little apart from the others looking grim and inaccessible. Her stomach clenched itself nastily.

It was the crunch of her tyres on gravel that dragged Luc from his reverie.

He turned and narrowed his gaze against the grey glare, attempting to make out the taxi's occupant. The graceful curve of cheek and neck he glimpsed beneath the hat brim looked youthful and extremely feminine. Surely…

No, it couldn't be Manon. She wouldn't have the gall to come *here,* flaunting her condition.

Shari got out, not sure she could trust her legs to support

her. As the taxi drove away she stood on the stone apron before the chapel, an alien in a foreign land. All eyes turned to stare at her.

Shari *felt* the instant Luc recognised her. A tremor jolted through his tall frame that communicated itself to her at a deeply visceral level. For whole seconds he stared at her, the curious intensity blazing in his dark eyes paralysing her where she stood.

He started towards her.

Shari's heart accelerated, far too fast. It was the first time she'd seen him in daylight. How could she have forgotten how—how he was? He looked powerful and autocratic, the expression of his strong, lean face grave and intent. As he neared she tried not to focus on the stirring lines of his mouth. Oh, Lord. This was hardly the time to be reminded of how it felt to be kissed by that mouth, but as he approached her insides roared into a mad, uncontrollable rush.

'Shari.' He searched her face, then bent formally to kiss each of her cheeks.

She'd mentally prepared herself for this. She'd promised herself she wouldn't allow him to touch her, kiss her, even brush her cheek with his roughened jaw, let alone touch her with his gorgeous lips. But when it came to the crunch...

'*Bonjour*,' she breathed, barely able to stand on her marshmallow knees. She felt the backs of her eyes prick and was possessed by a despicable longing to cling to his lapels.

Though gentle, his dark velvet voice seared her nerves like a bow drawn across the strings of a cello. 'I am sorry for your loss.'

'Oh. Oh, yes. Thanks. I know. It's dreadful, isn't it? Same—same to you, of course.'

Amber glowed in the depths of his dark eyes as they searched hers. With chagrin she supposed he was looking for traces of the bruise.

'You must be desolated,' he said.

Was he serious? Was this more mockery?

He continued. 'I did not expect… When did you arrive? Why did you not say? Who are you with? Where are you sleeping?'

Beneath her silken finery her breasts all at once felt indescribably tender. Some of the insulting assumptions he'd made during their previous encounter flooded back with raw immediacy, and she found herself breathing rather fast.

'Perhaps you mean with whom.'

His eyes glinted. '*Comment?*' He tilted up one thick black brow. '*Vraiment*, it's coming back to me. How you are.'

How she *was,* though, seemed to wholly concentrate his attention, because he devoured her from head to toe, raking her ensemble with a wolflike, smouldering curiosity that eliminated the rest of the world from her awareness. At the same time, the smoothness of his deep voice was having its old hypnotic effect. She might have been walking with him through the shrubbery on a summer's night.

'You are very pale. Your *lips* are pale.' He examined them with an intense interest. 'And you are thinner.' His gaze swept over her, lingering a second longer than was necessary below her throat. 'Though not too thin, fortunately.'

Scandalously, her overly sensitive breasts swelled to push the boundaries even of this new bra, and she began to feel almost aroused.

Inappropriate. *Thoroughly* inappropriate.

All these conflicting sensations were making her giddy, but somehow she stayed upright and said things. Some things, at least.

As if in a dream she inclined her head. 'I'm sure you mean that as a compliment, though I have no idea what you expected. It's only been a couple of weeks.'

She realised she'd made a gross tactical blunder when the ghost of a smile touched his mouth and she caught a glimpse of his white, even teeth. 'Five weeks and three days, to be exact.'

'I wouldn't know,' she said crushingly. 'I haven't been counting.'

She had the disconcerting feeling that the slight twitch at the corner of his mouth signalled satisfaction. But what did he have to be satisfied about? Why did he think she'd come here? For him?

He gestured then to the fascinated onlookers, in particular to a couple of elderly women who were circling to view her narrowly.

'*Maman, Tante Marise, c'est Shari,*' he said. '*La fiancée de Rémy.*'

'*Ex*-fiancée,' Shari corrected hurriedly, but her words were lost in the babble as family members closed in around her and subjected her to a gamut of curiosity. Only thing was, their questions, arguments and observations were all for each other, not for her.

Not that she'd have understood them anyway. Their French was so rapid and idiomatic she could scarcely pick up a word.

Except for the term *fiancée*. That was being bandied about quite furiously.

The next thing she knew someone patted her, though stiffly. Then someone else murmured something to her about Rémy and gave her a kindly nod. More people spoke to her, some with increasing warmth until everyone, including a hearty uncle with a face not unlike a truffle, seemed to be hugging her, kissing her and calling her *ma pauvre* and *ma puce*.

CHAPTER SIX

SHARI had visualised herself sitting in the rear of the chapel, alone, concealed perhaps by a marble pillar, a remote, mysterious, but essentially inconspicuous ghost. That wasn't how it went.

For one thing the ghost space was heavily occupied. Once inside that chapel, the passing of a life cut short was uppermost, whether or not Luc Valentin was present, overwhelmingly attractive and closely scrutinising her every move. As for being inconspicuous, the aunts had hustled Shari into the second front pew, across the aisle from Luc.

She'd always been far too emotional in stressful situations, and Rémy was all too powerfully present for comfort. And when Luc rose to deliver a brief eulogy, mainly in French, and a couple of people on her side of the aisle snivelled, Shari couldn't help shedding a couple of polite tears in sympathy.

The trouble was her tears took on a life of their own. It was so ridiculous. Once started they wouldn't stop. She cried so much about Rémy's stupid, selfish conceit, the agony he'd caused her and the humiliating things she'd let him get away with, that she filled up bunches and bunches of tissues. Though she tried to keep it as quiet as possible, her sobs probably sounded pretty heartbroken, when she wasn't *at all*. Face it, she wasn't all that sad.

But Rémy's family assumed she was. Those nearby patted and consoled her. Aunts, cousins, even the uncle shuffled seats to get near her and murmur comforting things until she gave in, laid her head on the truffle's shoulder and cried all down his suit.

Luc kept halting his speech to glower at her with a brow as dark as thunder. She could hardly blame him. When the worst of the embarrassing paroxysm had passed, he lowered his austere gaze to his text and continued on in English with a rather biting courtesy.

Shari supposed she should appreciate the consideration, although she doubted Rémy *was* the finest flower of the French nation, cut down in his prime by a heartless fate. She knew damned well what Luc meant to imply by that. A heartless *whore*.

And when he said a man was known by the quality of those who'd loved him, and went on to describe Rémy as a man who'd been possessed of earthly treasure and looked directly at her, she glared incredulously back through her tears. Oh, come *on*.

The man was a hypocrite. If she hadn't been so weepy and trembly from stress and the lack of a breakfast, she might have jumped up and said a few very gracious, dignified though at the same time rather terse things.

But the emotional toll of the past few weeks chose that critical moment to suspend her freedom of choice. Once again, just when she wanted to be at her sophisticated best, she was overcome by a wave of nausea.

Without time even to fumble for a dry tissue, she sprang up and rushed for the entrance, stumbled outside into the chill air and retched into a flower pot.

Nothing much came up. How could it? Nothing had gone down.

Sweating and gasping, as the last wrenching spasm subsided, she noticed a pair of masculine, highly polished leather shoes standing nearby. It occurred to her, even in her woeful state, they looked as if they'd been handmade by some Italian master.

'Are you better?' Luc's concerned voice broke through her humiliation and distress. 'Can you stand?'

'Of course,' she gasped. 'I'm fine.' She straightened up, grateful to feel his strong hand under her tottery elbow, and blotted her upper lip and forehead with a tissue. Foraging in her bag for another, she came across the bottle of cola. God bless the Hôtel du Louvre. Unscrewing the cap, she took a swig and turned aside to discreetly rinse her mouth. 'Excellent,' she panted, applying a tissue to her lips. 'I'm just a little empty. I haven't had any breakfast.'

'*Elle n'a pas pris de petit déjeuner*!' an excited voice relayed from close at hand.

'*Comment! Pas de petit déjeuner*?'

Until that ripple of concern about her non-breakfast electrified the crowd, Shari hadn't really noticed people streaming from the chapel and regrouping. Some had positioned themselves quite near to her and Luc, and were scrutinising her every move.

From under her chic *chapeau*, Tante Laraine in particular was watching her with an expression Shari couldn't quite interpret. Well, how would she? It was a very French expression. Though encountering the woman's disconcertingly shrewd gaze a second time, Shari corrected that analysis. A very *womanly* expression.

She wished she could melt through the stonework. Didn't these people understand a woman's need to retch in private? Several of them seemed anxious to remedy her plight, talking rapidly about taking her somewhere and plying her with food and blankets. Judging by the offers and counter-offers one relative tossed to another, and all with cool determined smiles, she gathered there was some sort of a polite contest under way.

Tante Marise for one was warmly insistent that Shari should go home with her and try a little *bouillon* and an egg.

Luc frowned at that and shook his head, instantly quashing the idea. The uncle bounded forward with an offer, but at a cool steel glance from Luc the words died on the old boy's lips and he retreated.

Then Tante Laraine intervened. Shari thought she could detect her resemblance to her son. While austerely gracious, this Laraine exuded a certain authority. Shari gathered the matriarch was strongly in favour of whisking her *chez Laraine* and feeding her some energising *chocolat.*

Luc, however, seemed even less keen on his mother having first shot at Shari. '*Non,*' he said ruthlessly. '*Pas du chocolat.*' He murmured something to hold them all at bay, then put his arm around Shari and held her close against his lean, powerful body.

'Come. You are shivering. We need to get you out of here.'

'Oh, but...' she quavered, regretting the *chocolat.* Even the *bouillon.* Now that her nausea had passed she really was quite cavernously empty. The egg would have been heaven. And if it had come with some hot buttered toast... 'I—I—I haven't properly expressed my condolences.'

He gave her a sardonic glance. 'I believe you have made your feelings perfectly clear. *Parfaitement.*'

It was glaringly apparent from his tone that the French despised a show of excess emotion. Shari cursed herself for her weakness. On top of everything else he thought was wrong with her, she had to keep giving into this crass emotionalism. It just had to stop.

Unexpectedly, a ray of watery sun pierced the grey world and lit the amber depths of his dark eyes, their glow sizzling through her bloodstream.

Luc steered her across to the first of several long, sleek limos that had silently drawn up in the last few minutes, and she went without resistance. Waving the driver back to the wheel, he opened the rear door for her himself and urged her inside. Shari sank into the warmth, grateful for the comfort.

She waited until he'd given his instructions to the driver and was settled at the other end of the wide seat before impressing him with her serene dignity.

'I'm sorry,' she said stiffly. 'I don't usually make such a spectacle of myself. I don't know what got into me. I feel— *mortified* to have embarrassed everyone.'

'No need to apologise.' A tinge of amusement momentarily relieved the saturnine severity of his expression. 'They loved it. They'll talk about it for months.'

She flushed. Though she kept her voice low, it still sounded fraught and emotional. She couldn't seem to control that. 'Heaven only knows what they think of me. I'm surprised they were so kind.'

His voice, on the contrary, was silky smooth. 'Why wouldn't they be kind? It is clear you are the very model of a grieving *fiancée*.'

She drew in a breath. Her voice grew all throaty and she was dangerously close to another bout of the waterworks. 'You know very well—I told you—I'm *not* a fiancée. Rémy and I broke up. I didn't even like him in the end. I despised him. Why must you taunt me? Are you always so cold and judgemental towards women?'

He flushed darkly. A muscle moved in his lean cheek. 'I don't believe so. That is not how I feel when I think of you. Far from it. But I'm naturally—surprised. You despised him, yet you have made this very long journey to say goodbye to him. And now to show such—*emotion*.'

'Well, but it was all so overwhelming, I just… Wouldn't *you* feel sad to say goodbye to someone you once loved?' She turned to look at him.

Through the smudged mascara her aquamarine gaze pierced Luc. An unpleasant knowledge solidified in his brain and skewered him straight through his gut. It hadn't mattered whether or not she'd liked the bastard. She'd loved him.

He said tightly, 'I can't imagine being sad about someone

who—violated the rules of civility. But I believe there are women who love certain men—whatever they do.'

A flicker of pain disturbed the cool green sea of her irises. She made a small, defensive gesture that sent a pang through Luc. The moment they'd shared at her front door flooded back to him with sharp immediacy. What an insensitive fool he was to bring that up now. He was handling this so badly. *Dieu*, was he jealous of a dead man?

'I doubt they do,' she said quietly. 'I think that's a myth.' The pride and earnestness in her voice touched him in some susceptible spot. 'Women fall in love then out of it, but some remain trapped by circumstances. That has never applied to me. It *could* never.' He watched her slim hands twist. The hat brim prevented him from seeing more than a section of cheek, an exquisite curve of chin.

His blood stirred with a sharp and bittersweet desire. He closed his eyes. She was here now, overwhelmingly present. Not a dream, not a fantasy. Whether he wanted it or not, yearning had him in its grip.

He sought for something to say to soften his former harshness. '*Très bon*. Men too can find themselves trapped. Passion is a dangerous thing. It can—drag you in.' She lanced him with her clear green gaze and he caught his breath. 'Not recommended for ones' health.'

'No,' she agreed, lowering her lashes. 'If only it were possible to consider your health at the time, no one would ever take the risk.' She hesitated. 'I—I…I'm sorry about the night you phoned. I know you meant to be kind.'

'I woke you from your sleep?' She nodded. He studied her face. 'You were angry.'

'Yes, well… It was a difficult time. I'm sorry.'

'Don't apologise. I phoned because I longed to hear your voice.'

Shari looked sharply at him, her heart revving up. His eyes

were scorching hot and were having quite a dizzying effect. Could he really talk as if nothing had happened?

This was no time for desire an hour after she'd farewelled Rémy. And hadn't Luc made it clear what he thought of her? Did he assume she was ready to ride that thorny road with him again? Had he *forgotten* what had happened after their boathouse tryst?

She started unsteadily, 'I don't know why you think I came all this way, Luc...'

'Then tell me. Why did you?' His dark eyes were compelling, alert, and at the same time so searingly sensual.

'For Emilie, of course. To—honour her loss. Pay our family's respects. And to—to acknowledge the love I once had for Rémy. Naturally.'

His gaze flickered over her, searching, intent. Then he lifted his shoulders in a gentle gesture. 'I always wonder when someone gives many reasons for doing something *grande* if they only really have the one. The one they wish to conceal from themselves.'

Her heart made a maniacal skitter. What? Did he think it had to do with him? Did the guy think one little encounter had affected her that deeply?

'And what do you suppose it to be?' She smiled in mocking disbelief. 'The one I need to conceal?'

His dark gaze was mercilessly direct. '*Bien sûr*, you came to see me.'

She gasped. Before she could deny it he curled his fingers under her chin and took her mouth in a fierce, highly sexual kiss. After the initial paralysed instant, her body sprang into tingling life. An erotic charge electrified her blood, her nerve fibres, her tender intimate tissues, as if this and this alone were her *raison d'être*.

Who said she couldn't communicate adequately in French? It was clear now all she'd ever needed was the inspiration. Luc

Valentin's hand merely had to caress her kneecap and slide up under her skirt and she burst into flame.

All right, she was bad. Bad in every way, but he felt *so good*. The delicious sinful pleasure of him thrilled through her and inflamed her every wanton molecule.

Sadly, just when she was ready to crawl onto his lap and express her appreciation more fulsomely for them both, he broke away. Drawing back, he studied her, his dark eyes beneath their thick black brows smouldering and amused.

'Good. Some colour in your cheeks.'

She felt herself flush. She supposed those cool, insolent words were intended to convey his macho self-possession. But to the sensitive ears of the guilt-ridden woman, the slightly thickened texture of his voice was a welcome giveaway. Luc Valentin was affected by her. Strongly affected.

'That was hardly appropriate,' she said breathlessly, patting down her suit and adjusting her hat. '*Now*. Of *all times*. Aren't you ashamed?'

'No. I would say—triumphant.'

Too shocked for words, she stared speechlessly at him, and he laughed and kissed her *again*. She was struggling for more words to express her discomfort at this bold exploitation of her weakened state, when the limo noticeably slowed.

Paris in all its glory had been flowing by—cafés, bridges, palaces, La Seine—and she'd barely had a chance to take in a thing. Now here they were at the city's throbbing heart. Even as she looked they drew up before a palace with ivory awnings over its several entrances.

'Where is this? Where are you taking me?' Straining, she narrowed her eyes to read the inscription on the nearest.

'To breakfast.'

A single word, emblazoned in a flowing script, adorned the graceful awning.

Ritz.

CHAPTER SEVEN

THE Ritz was the perfect antidote to an ordeal. The beauty, the food, the luscious notes of a string ensemble wafting on the air… Even the silk-festooned windows in their own lavish way declared the hotel's sincere desire to swaddle the emotionally gouged woman in loving and soul-restoring luxury.

There was a placard in the reception area announcing that the hotel was soon to close its doors for a major renovation and refurbishment. Shari prayed fervently they wouldn't change a thing.

The bathroom alone was an oasis of tranquillity, though she nearly freaked when she saw herself in the mirrors. Her face was blotchy, the tip of her nose red from all the bawling, and her mascara reminiscent of a bad Hallowe'en hangover. She looked a fright. How could Luc have wanted to kiss her?

She repaired the damage with the emergency kit at the bottom of her bag. Then, refreshed and reconstituted, she floated to join him in the restaurant. After all the emotion, she'd arrived on a tremulous smiley plateau where everything looked hazily beautiful. Especially the dark-eyed man drinking coffee and texting someone on his mobile.

Kill that thought. After all she'd gone through over him, was she to just fall into his arms? Was it always to be the same old thing? Shari Lacey, unable to resist a handsome Frenchman? Another one she knew little about and would be insane to trust?

He glanced up as she approached and his eyes shimmered,

inciting an excited clench in her insides. Then, just to mess with her defences, he rose and pulled out a chair for her.

She sat down, that car kiss still tingling through her nerve sockets. Somehow she would have to take a stand. Lay her position on the line before events rocketed out of control. Before she did.

He resumed his chair, his long lanky posture so relaxed and unbothered by anything he'd done to her in that limo it was a damned disgrace.

She steeled herself not to be affected, weakened or seduced. 'It's very good of you to bring me here, Luc. Very generous, but...' His brows twitched up. 'I—I—I think I should make it clear to you that anything of a-a sexual nature that may have happened between us in Sydney was a one-off. We agreed then it was a mistake, and... Well, so much has happened, and... As far as I'm concerned the whole thing should be wiped from our minds.'

He nodded along with her words as she spoke, though she noticed a certain tension infuse his gorgeous limbs. Then he lifted one quizzical brow. 'Ah. You think I should forget about meeting you at Emilie's?'

'I do. We should both forget it.'

'So then...' His black lashes flicked tauntingly downwards. A silky note entered his voice. 'You wish me to forget Emilie's garden?'

She eyed him carefully. What in particular might he be remembering about the garden? The last thing she needed to be reminded of was how easily she'd succumbed to that dark stroll into the shrubbery. 'I'm—surprised you even remember the garden.'

His eyes gleamed in reminiscence. 'Are you? But it was so pleasant, *d'accord*? In the dark, with all the fragrances and the moonlight.' His long fingers toyed idly with his spoon. The same fingers that had recently toyed with parts of her.

'You must remember the moonlight.' Her nerve jumped. 'The harbour lights.'

'Where are we going with this?' Although she knew where he was headed with it, all right.

He leaned forward, a lazy smile playing on his sexy mouth. 'I think you know where. Where else but to the boathouse? You're not expecting me to forget the *boathouse, chérie, n'est-ce pas?*'

'Well, I've forgotten it. As far as I'm concerned, nothing about it was very memorable.'

He threw back his head and laughed. He looked so handsome, with amusement illuminating his face and the light dancing in his eyes, a wave of hot and bitter frustration swept her. He had no right to be so attractive and to mock her. *He* was the one who'd found the magic moments shameful and made her feel like a disgrace to womanhood.

Luckily the waiter arrived just then, or she might have snatched up the coffee pot and whacked Luc over the head with it.

Controlling her annoyance, she turned her full attention to the menu, consulting earnestly with the waiter, feeling Luc's lazy glance scorch her face, throat and hands.

Everything enshrined on the list sounded delicious, but in the end she confined herself to ordering a spoonful of gentle, soothing yoghurt, along with some strawberries claimed to have been washed in morning dew. To follow she requested the buttery scrambled eggs, waiving both the caviar garnish and the champagne to wash them down.

Well, she had to show some respect for her stomach. It felt fine now, but who knew when it might rear up again in revolt?

While she enjoyed her yoghurt, Luc reflected on the effect their encounter had left on him. He still thought of it. No wonder he'd followed her home like a madman. *Nom de Dieu,* he was only flesh and blood. Would he ever forget holding her in his arms in that dark, sea-salty place? Her throaty little cries as he buried himself in her moist heat?

As he watched her soft lips close over a strawberry his blood stirred unbearably.

His underclothes tightened and he had to exert careful control over his voice. 'How—long do you plan to stay?'

'A couple of days. Tomorrow I thought I might visit the *Musée D'Orsay.* I fly home the day after that.'

Every sinew in his body tensed in utter rejection of that ludicrous plan. But outwardly he controlled the reaction. 'But how will you see Paris?'

'Well, I—I haven't come for a sightseeing tour, have I?'

She raised her glass to her lips. As she swallowed he noticed the muscles contract in her satin throat. Without warning a rush of hot turgid blood raced to his groin. He forced himself to shift his agonised gaze to the wall, the window, the orchid in its vase. Everywhere, anywhere until he could trust his voice.

'That's—a very brief visit. Surely…you can transfer your flight to a future date?'

She shot him a glance. 'I'm not sure why I would do that.' He waited for the next flash of green, his breath on hold. 'I suppose…if I had a *reason*…'

He could think of a damned good one, but not one that was sayable. Surely she could feel the pulse as strongly as he? Why did things have to be so complicated with women?

'A reason to stay in Paris,' he mused aloud. 'Not many people in the world would find that a challenge.'

The sensual note in his voice registered in Shari's hearing. With his lashes at half mast she was reminded of a devious, smouldering wolf. Why should she find that so scarily thrilling? The dangerous little tongue of flame threatening to undo her licked deep.

Her scrambled eggs were set before her, moist, speckled with parsley, and accompanied by pale golden toast. The eggs melted on her tongue, while the hot chocolate might well have been the most divine ever to pass human lips.

Unusually for her, however, she didn't manage to clean up every last scrap. It was hard to concentrate her attention on even food when such a man was distracting her.

When the waiter returned to clear her dishes, she noticed Luc listening to her flowery praise of the chef, a smile lurking in his eyes.

'You were very kind,' he observed after the man had gone.

'Artists ought to be appreciated.'

'Artists like you?'

'Now who's being kind?'

He met her gaze, smiling in return, making her helpless heart somersault. 'I believe I have seen your book.'

She widened her eyes. 'Here? Honestly? *Here*?'

'*Oui*. In a bookshop. I happened to wander in and—there it was. I thought it was—' every nerve in her body held its breath in trembling hope '—so—beautiful.'

Oh, the relief. Her fearful heart glowed so fiercely she could have danced, sung and cried all at the same time. It didn't matter if he was sincere. Just that he was being kind. Just for that moment she loved him. Loved Luc Valentin with all her heart.

'Thanks.' Her smile burst through. 'It's always lovely not to be crushed.'

He grinned, then his face grew rather grave and he cleared his throat. '*Alors,* Shari, I do wish to express how...I—I—regret the way it ended in Sydney.'

'I'm glad you brought it up,' she said tensely, thinking of all those sleepless nights of futile yearning, knowing he thought so badly of her. The injustice of the things he said. Her mortification when he caught her at her most naked. Her anger and misery, and... *Oh, God.* Maddening, unsatisfiable desire. 'I—I don't think you know how those things you said—*hurt* me. I...'

He blinked, then concealed his eyes behind his lashes. He said stiffly, 'Perhaps you took it all too much to heart.'

She sat back and smiled coolly. 'Which part?' She could feel herself start to tremble. 'The part where you didn't believe me? Where you accused me of being a dishonourable slag? Or the bit when you followed me home like a stalker?' She kept on smiling, though her heart was suddenly working like a piston.

A tinge of colour darkened his bronzed cheek. 'Perhaps it seemed that way. But you must see that at the *time*...'

'*No*.' She disciplined herself to keep her voice low. 'At the *time*, Luc, I was not a liar. If I committed any crime it was a crime against myself. My own code of behaviour—and—and—*safety* in offering the pleasure of my body to a man I didn't know and couldn't trust.'

'Trust?' He spoke so sharply she jumped. '*Vraiment*, this was a matter of honour. I was afraid you—might still be involved with *my cousin*.'

Startled by his vehemence, she compressed her lips, but, unable to hold in *some* defence of herself, she burst into a fierce whisper. 'If I *had* been do you think I'd have betrayed him? Are you still thinking of me like that? As a—a *whore*? Oh, it's too much. Too much.' She threw down her napkin and rose to her feet, emotion rising faster in her than high tide at Bondi.

'Shari, no, no, I don't think that. Please.' He sprang up and took her arms, his eyes earnest and intent. 'I have never *said* that. I thought you were a very passionate and beautiful woman in the midst of a—a complex situation. I could see we needed to discuss it and—analyse it like rational adults. Why do you think I followed you home?'

'Oh, *why*? Obvious. You thought you could sweet-talk your way into my bed. And is that why you've brought me here to the Ritz? You're hoping to try your luck *again*?'

He looked shocked. His handsome face assumed such a gravely wounded expression she wondered if she'd been unjust.

'That is a—disappointing suggestion.'

It was a suggestion that had only just surfaced in her mind, but once it did, it took root.

He was shaking his head in austere denial of the charge when her glance fell on his mouth. Paradoxically, against all reason and logic, in total betrayal of herself and the sisterhood of women, she was seized with an irresistible impulse to ravage that stirring mouth, to tease those sternly compressed lips apart with her tongue and drink in every last masculine drop of Luc Valentin.

At the same time her nipples, the tender vibrant tissues between her legs tingled and flamed with a violent, feminine yearning impossible to repress.

As though he were divining her lustful state a piercing gleam lit Luc's eyes. He lifted his brows. A subtle change came over his demeanour. 'Shh, shh, *chérie*.' His voice became silky smooth. 'It has been a stressful morning. Sit down again for a minute. Come, now.'

She glanced about. Naturally, there were a few interested parties straining to catch every word—a couple of princes, several duchesses with their beaux and a sheikh—though none of them seemed to be goggling with as much curiosity as they would have if this scene had been taking place in a Sydney restaurant.

In a fever of confusion, she resumed her place. How could she desire someone who'd caused her such distress? How could she want to bite his bronzed neck, drink his blood and eat him alive?

He leaned forward, his lean face stern, his eyes searing her with an urgent intent. 'We need to talk. Settle this somewhere private, where we can be alone.' Suddenly he was radiating energy, like a ship's captain taking charge of a serious aquatic catastrophe. He grasped her hand and squeezed. 'Give me two minutes—I'll arrange a quiet corner.' He stood up. 'Will you be OK here? *Oui*? Now, don't leave.'

He gave her a firm look to hold her there, then strode away.

Shari closed her eyes. What was wrong with her? She'd been angry with him for so long, now as soon as she met him again, she felt— Oh, face it. Thrilled to be with him. Every-thing he said—even the bits that outraged her—every small nuance was etching itself on her heart.

He was devastating her again. The last time a Frenchman made her feel this way... Look what happened! She should have walked out. Summoned a taxi and flown back to the Hôtel du Louvre. Taken off her hat, crawled into bed and eased her mad and insatiable desires as best she could in the time-honoured way.

But his electrifying squeeze was still burning her hand. And she needed to hear what he had to say. Maybe he would apolo-gise so sincerely she could honourably forgive him.

Forgive him and...

Anyway, it would be a shame to take off the hat before it was absolutely necessary.

To evade more vulgar curiosity, she swanned to the bath-room and, armed with her toothkit from the plane, managed to give her teeth a good minty scrub.

She emerged in time to see Luc return from the direction of the reception area. He walked with such confident mascu-line authority, such athletic energy in his long limbs, she felt a flame of longing sear deep inside her.

He caught sight of her and changed course, strolling across to smoothly, possessively take her arm. 'Come.'

Slipping her bag onto her shoulder, she savoured the erotic graze of his suit fabric on her skin. 'Have you—found a place where we can talk?'

'No problem.' His dark gaze dwelled smoulderingly on her face. 'They assure me it will be very, very quiet.'

He ushered her into a lift and pressed the button for the fifth floor.

'Have you...?' She turned to gaze at him. 'Have you ever read *The Pursuit of Love*?'

He glanced keenly at her, eyes gleaming. '*The Pursuit of...*?'

She tried not to show it, but she was breathing so fast her

breasts were rising and falling like twin peaks during a major quake. '*Love*. The heroine finds herself stranded at the Gare du Nord without any money. This Frenchman strolls by…'

His eyes sharpened. 'A Frenchman?'

'Yes. A tall, very sexy, very wicked duke. He persuades her to go home with him and he…'

He lifted his brows. '*Oui*? What does he do?'

'Oh. Well, er…' She stared at his mouth and said breathlessly, 'I may need to revisit that part of the story to remind myself.'

His eyes burned. The air crackled with a tension that singed her very nerve endings.

The doors slid open and he guided her along a hushed corridor until they came to a door numbered 514. He slipped the card into the lock.

The door opened to a light, elegant foyer.

Shari blinked. 'But—this is a room.'

He shrugged. '*Bien sûr*.'

She walked in, tingling with a primitive anticipation. The room was spacious, with beautiful panelled walls and moulded ceilings at least four metres high. The carpet under her feet felt as deep and soft as a cloud. The further in she walked, the more there was to steal her breath.

A fine antique tapestry. Paintings, sparingly placed. Silken panels in shades of carmine and duck-egg blue, reflecting the gorgeous colours in the Persian rugs. Then there were the double windows with their long sensuous drapes, the moulded fireplace and heartbreakingly exquisite Louis Quinze furnishings.

What was most significant to her eye, though, and zinged through her like an ocean wave, was beckoning through an open door. A magnificent king-sized bed, arrayed with plump, inviting pillows set atop a charming counterpane.

'Oh,' she said faintly. 'It's a suite.'

'As private as we could wish for, surely.' He strolled across to the windows and gazed down into the street. She noted a sudden tension in the set of his wide shoulders. A suspenseful tension that communicated itself to her and electrified the very room.

He turned to her, and her lungs seized. Beneath his heavy brows his dark eyes shimmered with a molten, lascivious intent.

He said softly, 'Would you care to take off your hat?'

She tingled all over. Her heart was thundering. Her feet started to move, and as he strode swiftly across to her she practically flung herself at his hard body. She threw her arms around his neck and met his fierce, thirsty impassioned kisses with reckless disregard for any moral or overruling principle.

Her hat landed on the sofa, and while she tore at his shirt and unbuckled his belt to open his trousers he dropped her suit on the rug, unclipped her bra and stripped her bare.

The lithe beauty of his lean, muscular body, never seen, only felt, was as thrilling as her most fevered imaginings.

She gasped as his powerful erection rose in proud and gorgeous majesty. But her questing hands barely had time to stroke, squeeze and relish the prime virile beauty before he fell upon her nakedness like a hungry beast.

He kissed her breasts, licked her engorged nipples, blazed a trail of greedy kisses down to her navel and below.

Then he dropped to his knees. Embracing her thighs, he ravaged her curls with his mouth, then pushed her to the sofa. She trembled with sheer excitement. Parting her thighs, he paused a moment to feast his eyes, then, while she whimpered for blissful joy, bent his dark head between her legs and licked the tickly velvet. Tingles of erotic pleasure radiated through her in dark liquid waves.

When he took her clit between his gorgeous lips and sucked—heaven on earth—her panting moans turned to sobs of pure ecstasy.

With an actual blossoming orgasm, she cried out in disbelief when he drew away, leaving her hanging on an edge. 'Don't stop *now*. Please, please, keep…'

But, ignoring her complaints, he stood up to draw a small package from his jacket pocket. Swiftly he sheathed himself, then, taking her hands, pulled her off the sofa and into his arms. In the stumbling rush to the bedroom, she hooked her arms around his neck, her legs around his hips.

There was a thrilling urgency to his haste. Devouring her mouth with what could only be called passionate savagery, he plunged inside her even before she hit the mattress.

Once on it, she gave herself up to the heavenly friction. And he was a master. He filled her so full her body exploded with light with his every sinuous movement. Rocking her into an urgent pulsing rhythm, he ignited rivers of magic in her flesh. Fireworks infused her every capillary.

And just like the first time, the fierce and hungry fervour in his eyes and the athletic synchronicity of their bodies rocketed her passion to an explosive and fantastic climax.

Long after her wild, appreciative cries subsided, she floated, eyes closed for seconds, minutes, maybe even hours on a cloud of blissful contemplation.

Vindicated. Vindicated as a woman.

When her heartbeat was back to near normal Luc lay on his back, lashes half the way down to reveal only slits of eyes, like a slumberous lion after a killing.

She smiled. 'That was fantastic.'

'Likewise,' he said gravely. 'You are *formidable*. So passionate.'

'Thanks.' She blushed. Her heart glowed at the recognition. Positively beamed through her chest wall. 'And you know, it felt *amazing*. It's rare for me to ever feel so—hot. It was truly liberating. It must have been the reaction to all the stress.'

'I'm so happy the stress worked for you,' he said smoothly, his eyes glinting.

She guessed Frenchwomen, being so mysterious and sophisticated, didn't confess their feelings after sex.

'Well, there was that other time too, of course. My first actual...' She screeched to a halt in the bare nick of time.

His lifted an eyebrow. 'Your first...?'

'Boathouse. I recall feeling pretty well piping hot there.'

Heavens, time to shut the heck up. She'd brushed pretty close to giving away her fatal flaw. Knowing she was back in the orgasmic hot zone though, so to speak, was fantastically motivating. After her rocky start this morning, she could hardly believe she'd achieved this marvellous and formidable feeling of heavenly freedom and pleasantness.

After a moment he said, 'But you must have known many other occasions when you felt so piping hot, having been engaged?'

'Oh, sure. Of course, of course.' She gave her hand an airy wave. 'Although...' She hesitated, and added with a self-conscious flutter, 'Well... The conditions can't always be perfect, can they?'

'They can't?'

'Well, I don't know how a man feels, but I guess a woman needs to feel—admired.'

He drew his brows in a frown. 'But Rémy admired you, d'accord? He asked you to marry him.'

'Not marry, exactly. Just—to get engaged. Marriage was to be in the distant future. He wanted to establish D'Avion in Australia properly first.'

He laughed softly. 'Tiens.'

'I think what he really meant was he wanted to romance every woman in Sydney first.' She laughed sadly, though it was a rueful sadness now, not the broken-hearted one it had once been. Rueful, she supposed, for her part in everything that had gone wrong. Sad, because Rémy, having hurt so many people, would now never even have the chance to redeem himself.

Luc leaned over and kissed her. 'He was a fool. He didn' know what he had.'

'You're not wrong.' She smiled.

He took her in his arms and kissed her again, more deeply this time. Quite emotionally in fact. It was really very stirring and beautiful. And the graze of his chest hair against her breasts was so erotic, she felt as if she was in the most perfect location on the planet.

When the kiss ended they drew apart, then laughed a little embarrassedly at their intensity. 'Who'd have thought we'd have ended up here?' she said, grinning.

'Not me. When I saw you this morning I thought I was hallucinating.'

'*I* thought I was going to faint.'

'I have that effect,' he said modestly, laughing when she gave him a playful punch. He stacked the pillows up behind his head. 'But I can't understand why you agreed to be engaged to *him*? What was it about him?'

'Dunno. I was a fool. Naive, I s'pose. He seemed—charming. Exciting. Romantic.'

'*Romantic*?' His face expressed Gallic disbelief.

She hardly wanted to admit she was a Georgette-Heyer-style Regency heroine with deep-held fantasies about marrying a sexy earl. Not that Rémy was in any way an earl, though he'd *claimed* to have one in his family.

'Well, he *was* my first Frenchman. All my girlfriends thought he was really, really hot. I felt so lucky…I was sort of swept along, I guess. For a while.' She compressed her lips. 'I s'pose in fairness he was too. And Em was so thrilled. I *think* she was relieved he'd finally decided to settle down.' She grimaced. 'The irony of that. He was about as settled down as Casanova. I've sure learnt my lesson. Settling down is highly overrated.'

'Be careful who you settle down *with* next time.'

She squeezed his pleasingly hard bicep. 'Haven't you been listening, *monsieur*? There won't *be* a next time.'

'How can you say so? There'll be some good solid guy searching the world for you even now.'

She felt a sharp pang. He wasn't thinking of himself in that regard, then. She said rather tartly, 'Tsk, tsk. Poor him. He can wash his own socks and cook his own dinners. From now on I intend to be a woman of affairs, living for the good times.'

Luc appraised her face. She was smiling, but there were shadows in her eyes. As on that night in Paddington, that impulse seized him. That desire to drive away those shadows and wipe the darkness from her life.

He'd have laughed at himself if it hadn't been for a flash of his return to his hotel that night. Blindly negotiating the city streets, scored with longing and regret. Guilt. One of the most rugged journeys of his life.

At the time he'd burned to snatch her out of harm's way. But, of course, the cold light of morning had reminded him of his reasons to board the plane, Rémy's theft from the company being foremost.

He frowned. 'Was it—so bad?'

She glanced quickly at him. 'Not at first. But—gradually. As the gloss wore off. I think you've guessed...' She dropped her eyes. 'He wasn't always—very nice.'

'He was—violent?'

There was a tiny tremor at the corner of her mouth, and he felt something inside him tighten.

'Not with his fists, no, except that one time at the end when he was desperate to find his passport. He was just cruel—in little careless ways. Things he said. About me, about Neil. Sometimes he'd touch me, pull my hair in a joke, though always a little bit too hard. Not like a person who loved you.'

Luc lay frowning, his pulse beating hard with the increase in his blood pressure. His fists had bunched involuntarily. It was a good thing Rémy was where he was now, or he'd have felt this fierce need to go after him and teach him something about civility and decency. Not that more violence would ever be the answer.

He glanced at her downcast face. 'I had heard—Rémy's papa wasn't very kind. There were rumours in the family...'

'I know. Emilie mentioned it once. But I never expected— *that*.'

'Of course not.'

Perhaps unlucky Rémy had been poorly conditioned as a child, but... Luc burned to think of a man treating *any* woman this way. To enjoy hurting Shari... How could the guy have? Examining the fragile lines of her face, he guessed there was more she could have told. Far more.

Caution sounded a warning note in his brain. Perhaps it was better he didn't know those things. His rational mind told him the more a man learned about a woman, the more he saw into her, the deeper he sank into the emotional quicksand. Already his responses to her were out of all proportion. Way out. Just one morning with her and he was dangerously close to relaxing his guard completely.

Had he forgotten where it could all end?

Shari felt a tension in the lengthening silence. Maybe she'd said too much. She could almost hear his brain analysing the evidence, weighing it all up.

'Anyway, enough about my little case,' she said lightly. 'Everyone's break-up is painful, is it not? *C'est la vie*, hey, *monsieur*?' With a rueful smile she reached up and rubbed her knuckle over his cheek. 'Haven't we all loved and lost?'

His expression lightened almost at once. 'You are right. My last lover preferred a famous movie star to *me*. Can you imagine?' He made a comical face, and she joined him in a laugh.

As the room grew silent again she wondered if there was a certain brooding flavour to the atmosphere. 'She must be insane,' she murmured.

He grimaced, then his face lightened to a smile. 'I thought of you every day, after we parted.'

'About the bruise?'

He frowned. 'Not that. About you. How beautiful you are. How—original.' She hardly believed it. Even so, her mouse heart thrilled to its little rodent core. 'Every hour…of every day.'

'And I thought of *you* every day. I wanted to murder you. I wanted to make you *sorry*. I wanted to put my hands around your strong, beautiful neck and…'

A flame lit his dark eyes. 'Come here.' He reached for her. He whispered the words against her mouth. 'I was sorry. I *am* sorry. Now I want you to forget—*everything*.'

This time his passion was darker, more fervent, more tender. A fierce and ardent light glowed in his eyes as he rocked her, filled her and pleasured her until she was blazing with light and higher than the moon.

And she did forget. She forgot everything in existence except the world of his arms, his passionate mouth, his beautiful, hard, thrusting body, the fierce heat in his eyes.

While Paris ticked over outside and the day drew on, their lips grew raw with kissing, their bodies sated. With exhaustion in view, Luc dragged up the sheet to cover them. Shari lay face to face with him, languorous eyes to eyes.

Gently, he pushed her hair from her face. 'Two days is too short. You should stay longer.'

'What for?' She traced the outline of his mouth with her finger.

'For this.'

Her heart skipped a heavy beat. What was this? This mad, uncontrollable need to hold him to her and never let him go. When had she ever known this intense mutual tenderness and passion? She wanted to run outside and shout it to the world. Luc Valentin wanted her. He was asking her to stay in Paris. In his apartment.

She said carefully, 'I only have my hotel room for the three nights. They mightn't be able to let me keep it longer.' She held her breath.

'*Bien sûr*, stay here.'

'*Here*?' A pang of disappointment, so intense it was scary, cut through her. She dragged up an empty laugh while inwardly she cringed. 'Oh, I don't think so.'

Oh, how she'd misinterpreted.

'I can't tempt you? A week at the Ritz? You can do your sightseeing while I'm at work, then in the evenings… More sightseeing.' He lifted his brows suggestively.

She concealed her gaze from him. 'You can tempt me to some more of those scrambled eggs. I'm hungry enough to eat everything in this room.' What a *fool* she must be. What a needy, susceptible fool. A few sweet words and she was ready to believe anything.

Imagine if she did stay the week. In no time she'd be dreaming of a future. Deluding herself, listening for clues of his intentions. Laying herself open to disappointment.

Hello, heartbreak, her old BFF.

She showered with him while waiting for the food, then, wrapped in a peach towelling bathrobe, shared the feast Luc had ordered.

'I'll have to put some clothes on soon,' he said, sighing. 'We'll need more protection if I am to keep you happy. Mustn't risk anything going wrong.'

She stared down at her scramble. A paralysing thought surfaced in her mind. Perhaps it had always been there, just below her consciousness. Since the boathouse. Since the PMT that hadn't eventuated into anything. The nausea on the plane. No, there'd been more even before that.

With too much to think about—Luc, Rémy, Emilie, the twins, booking her journey, the dread and excitement at seeing Luc again—she'd allowed her body no room in her thoughts.

Too frightening to acknowledge, too catastrophic, the vague

and extreme possibility crystallised in her brain with ruthless digital clarity.

'No,' she said hollowly. 'It would be awful if anything went wrong.'

Her heart plunged in freefall.

CHAPTER EIGHT

Luc was on the move early, needing to attend to his office. Shari stayed in bed, waving away any suggestion of breakfast. 'I want to sleep a little more,' she said weakly from her pillow, knowing what would happen if she tried to sit up.

'Are you sure? Not even some *chocolat*?'

She only just repressed a shudder.

'Ah...if you are still wishing to visit the d'Orsay, I could collect you here at eleven.'

'Oh, right. The d'Orsay.' Though at that exact moment, pictures were not the first thing on her mind. 'Oh, so you—want to come too?'

His eyes veiled and he said carelessly, 'Unless you prefer to be alone when you look at pictures.'

She hated to hurt his feelings. 'No, no, not at all. I'd love you to come.' She should be able to fix herself up before then, one way or another. 'How about I meet you there? I'll enjoy finding my own way.'

He looked more closely at her, his brows drawing together. 'Are you feeling quite well?'

'Oh, heck yeah. Just tired. What would you expect?' She conjured up a grin.

'*Très bon*.' Smiling, he wrote down his mobile number for her, dropped a kiss on her forehead and left.

The second the door closed behind him, Shari dragged herself up and lunged for the bathroom. There was another ghastly attack, though she seemed to deal with it more briskly this time. Maybe she'd even get used to it. Panting, she screwed up her face. How fun to be a woman. The likely diagnosis loomed with a hopeless inevitability.

After showering and washing her hair, she felt slightly more human, if no braver. She dressed and took the lift down to the lobby.

The concierge directed her to a nearby pharmacy. Outside, in cruel mockery of her situation, the sun was daring to shine weakly, the sky having the crass insensitivity to glow with a pale, hopeful blue.

With a pregnancy testing kit burning a hole in her bag, Shari hurried back to the hotel and requested a taxi. Her own room at the Louvre felt more the place to face the moment of truth.

An hour later she sat on the smooth coverlet of her bed, hot and cold by turns. An initial bout of sheer panic and desperation had given way to something like bleak acceptance, though her brain was in a jumble. Did she *want* to be pregnant? Without a relationship to depend on?

Of course not. She couldn't do it. She was in no position to. Her mother had been left to raise her on her own, and look how hard their life had been. Never two cents to scrape together. Shoes that wore through the soles before they were replaced. Her mother working two jobs. If Neil hadn't been there as a support she didn't know how they'd have held together.

She supposed she'd always assumed she would have a child some day, but not until she had the man. Never, never without the man. She just didn't have that sort of courage and she was hardly in any financial position, with her career still in its shaky infancy.

One book published, and a tiny little advance for the next?

Another attack of panic gripped her as her conscience chimed in to taunt her. Too late, Shari. A child has started now. *Your...*

She broke out in a sweat. She needed to think. Focus on immediate practicalities. Like how to inform Luc.

Oh, God.

Whether to inform him.

A man who invited a woman to stay for a week—*in a hotel*—wasn't contemplating an ongoing relationship. She doubted if even his offer of the Ritz would stand once she told him. Everything would be over. He'd get rid of her fast.

Nothing like the prospect of a responsibility to cool a man's ardour.

Although… Although… Try to think straight, Shari. Luc was a man of the world. He would be sophisticated about it. Suggest the logical solution. Surely that would be for the best.

If only she hadn't been so ignorant about France. Knowing Rémy and Emilie had given her some insights, but Rémy was hardly likely to have been typical of Frenchmen.

Surely the French were very religious, *Notre Dame de Paris* and all that. If she told Luc, maybe he would insist she go through with it.

And what? Leave her stuck with a child and send her money every month?

The alternative was no less confronting. Her thoughts skittered towards movie images of the clinic waiting room and shied away again.

If only she had a friend she could talk to, right here, right now—Neil. If only she had her brother. He was on her side, no matter what, and at least in Australia she knew the rules. With such huge scary decisions to make, a strange country was not the place to be.

She considered phoning Em, but what was the point? She knew what Em would say. Anyway, Australia would be asleep now.

Whatever, she'd better be on that plane tomorrow.

Luc arrived at the Musée d'Orsay a few minutes before the appointed time. He strolled about before the entrance, enjoying the brisk air, avoiding tour groups and keeping his eye on the taxis that drew up to disgorge visitors.

He felt no concern about taking another day away from the office. *Zut*, he might even take a few more.

He glanced at his watch. A minute or two past the hour. Then some extra-sensory instinct alerted him and he glanced up. That dizzying swoosh as the breath caught in his lungs. She was on foot, strolling from the direction of the Pont Royal that crossed the river from the Tuileries.

She looked as casual and unFrench as any of the tourists queuing up for entry to the museum, wearing a trench over jeans and sneakers. Scarf carelessly knotted around her neck, her blonde hair rippling free. When she drew near a smile touched her mouth, fleetingly, then she grew serious again.

He narrowed his eyes. How pale she seemed.

When he kissed her, her cheeks felt cold against his lips. He slipped his hands inside her trench and drew her close, inhaling the sweet fragrance that enveloped her from head to toe. Desire quickened his blood. His mouth watered with the yearning to kiss her properly.

'Are you tired from walking? Or did I wear you out?'

Drawing back after a few blood-stirring seconds, her heart still thumping, Shari met his warmly sensual gaze. Like her, he'd changed clothes. He was clean-shaven and sexy in dark trousers and a black polo-neck with a dark brown leather jacket.

That electric current was tugging her, making her want him. Astonishing she could still feel that way when her tender places were in need of some respite from the action. And with *this*... How could she even *want* to feel like this now?

Madly though, like an addict, she did.

'It wasn't that far. I love to walk.' She showed him the map given her by the concierge at the Hôtel du Louvre. 'See? I wanted to see as much as I could before I fly away.' And maybe the exercise would do her good.

'But you aren't flying yet. You're staying a week. Two weeks.'

Two now? She lowered her gaze. 'We'll see.'

See how keen he would be when he knew. When she told him what was growing inside her and taking over her body, her life, the *world*. How would he handle such news? That moment in Sydney when he'd heard Rémy spoken of as her fiancé flashed into her mind. His reaction had been severe enough then, but that had been nothing like *this*.

Would he blame her? A bolt of pure panic made her hands and armpits moisten, and for a second she nearly reeled. Oh, God in heaven, she should get a grip. Luc wasn't the violent type. After yesterday and last night, how could she even think of comparing him with Rémy?

Examining her face, Luc felt the slightest twinge of anxiety. Surely she wasn't still thinking of boarding that flight? A petite woman shouldn't undertake such a harrowing journey again so soon. She still hadn't recovered from the first. Why else would she be so pale?

For the next two hours Shari wandered through the gallery in a turmoil of unreality. Staring blindly at work after exquisite work, she was unable to think of anything except—*it*. It was a mere embryo now, she supposed. Not much more than a few tiny little cells. With a face, already? How long would it take eyes, nose and lips to develop?

She wished she could dash somewhere private to look it up on the Internet. Maybe when she got back to the hotel. Find out the developmental stages. Despite everything, she was curious to at least see what it looked like.

She felt Luc send her a couple of searching glances, and realised she'd hardly said a word. She needed to clean up her act. This was no way for a grown woman to take charge of what was, after all, a perfectly normal though terrifying situation.

'What do you think?' he said, paused before a *Starry Night Over the Rhone*.

She tried to focus. The painting shimmered before her gaze, ablaze with passion and aspiration, hope and the purest joy in simple things. How could such a treasure have been created by someone in a far worse life predicament than she could ever contemplate?

Oh, she was such a coward. Tears swam into her eyes. 'It's— a dream. Magic. The *vibrancy* of it. You imagine you know about something, but when you're up close to it, in real life, and it's connected to *you* your entire perception changes. You suddenly realise fate has you in its sights, and you're helpless against nature. You're nothing. You thought you had power to control your life but...' Suddenly sensing his keen scrutiny, she stemmed the wild flow with a lurch of dismay.

What on earth had she been babbling?

'That's how *I* feel,' he exclaimed. 'It's as if Vincent knew exactly what was in my heart when he painted this picture. I am so pleased you feel the power of it too. But not surprised,' he added warmly. 'Not at all surprised.'

He put his arm around her and hugged her to him as if she was a precious thing. She smiled, relieved, so pleased to still be in accord with him, but underneath her glow her anxiety only intensified. He was warm *now*, so admiring, appreciative of her charms. Liking her. How would he feel when she told him? Would she see a swift and deadly turnaround?

Just imagining him turning cold and distant made her heart pang with dread.

'Are you feeling very well?' He was looking closely at her.

'Sure. Fine. Do you—do you visit here often?'

He continued to scrutinise her. 'Not so often now. Though I know it well, of course. If I'm in Paris at the weekends I like to visit the smaller galleries—ones out of the usual way of the tourists.'

'I'm a tourist,' she reminded him.

But she was thinking how little she knew of him. This tiny little minuscule face was unfurling, maybe resembling *his*...

She squashed that hysterical thought. Ridiculous when she knew zilch about the whole development thing, and anyway she had no idea what she was planning to do about it.

'What do you do at weekends when you aren't in Paris?'

He lifted his shoulders. 'Different things. My family have a little farm in the country. I visit there sometimes.'

'A farm? Is that where your mother lives?'

He smiled. 'Sometimes she goes there. Sometimes the Alps, or the beach, especially when Paris is too hot. But in winter she prefers her apartment.'

'And your father?'

'He lives in Venice.'

'Why Venice?'

He lifted quizzical brows at her. 'His lover lives there.'

She flushed. 'Forgive me for asking so many questions.' How crass she must have sounded. 'I feel as if you know everything about me and I know so little about you.'

He looked amused. 'Ask what you like.'

He looked relaxed enough, but all at once she felt shy. She knew she was bound to make a mess of framing the right questions. What were they, even? Where to start? There should be a manual available for the woman who was knocked up in a one-night stand.

She hesitated. 'Well, do you...? You mentioned your ex-fiancée. Manon—is it? Emilie told me a little bit about her.'

She sensed a sudden stillness in him. Then he said smoothly, 'She was not my *fiancée*.' He gave an insouciant shrug. 'We—had a looser arrangement than that.'

'Oh?'

She paused before a painting of a village church. Heavenly blue and the most glorious, joyous yellow she'd ever imagined possible. Honestly, all this beauty was playing so excruciatingly on her emotions, her eyes kept pricking. It was probably one of the symptoms. As if she needed any more.

She glanced at him. 'What of now? As of this moment. Do you have someone?'

Though he was amused, his eyes glinted. 'As of this moment I am here with you.'

She moistened her lips. 'Were you and she together—a long time? You and Manon?'

'Some years. Six. Seven.' His lashes swept down.

'Oh. That is a long time.' She felt surprised. She hadn't realised the relationship had been quite so—established. For a loose arrangement it seemed long. Whatever 'loose' meant.

A man who'd been in a seven-year relationship didn't seem like a man who fooled around, at any rate. She glanced speculatively at him. Would he have…?

Frowning, she moved on to the next picture. Pretended to examine it. 'I saw a picture of her. She's very beautiful. Emilie said she's renowned for her elegance and *chic*.'

'Did she?' His lip made a sardonic curl. 'I must thank Emilie for informing you so well. No doubt she told you about the dog.'

She glanced at him in surprise. 'No. She never mentioned a dog.'

'*Tiens*. I am grateful.'

Though if there was a dog, it was sounding far more domestic than she had imagined from her understanding of loose arrangements.

'Did you…?' She drew a breath. 'Did you never think of marrying her?'

His eyes veiled, then slid away. Suddenly he leaned forward to study a scene where some fully clothed men were picnicking by a stream with a naked woman. 'Do you not admire the artist's use of the light here? If I could only achieve this effect I believe I might be content for all time.'

Shari took a moment to digest the stunning snub. Maybe she should have expected it. Clearly, the intimacy of the bed did not translate to the museum. There were lines she must not cross.

Why, oh, why had she even *asked* him? It wasn't as if she

expected him to marry *her*. But that was what he would assume when she broke the news. He'd think she was looking to trap him in playing happy families.

Breaking into a sweat, she edged away from him.

Face it, it was clear he was still pretty raw about losing the beautiful woman. Well, it was only natural. Any guy's ego was bound to feel trashed if his girlfriend ran off with a movie idol.

Especially if the guy was still madly in love with her.

'Why are you wrinkling up your face and looking as if you tasted a lemon?' She started. Luc slipped his arms around her and kissed her ear. 'Is Renoir such a disappointment?'

She flashed him a rueful smile. 'Never. How could he be? To be honest I—I was feeling guilty. I think I've intruded, asking you things you don't care to discuss. I guess you're thinking those things some French people say about Australians.'

'What do they say?'

'Oh, you know. We're too open. Too—forward.'

He laughed easily. 'Who says that? Come, we will eat *déjeuner*. My mother wants to meet you properly. The family will be there.'

Shari's heart sank. 'Lovely.'

There was no sign of the limo. Luc ushered her to a neat little Merc parked in a nearby street. As soon as they were in the car, he pulled her into his arms and kissed her, a steamy, highly explorational clinch that sucked all the breath from her lungs and shut down her brain entirely. Responding to the sexual cue, her wanton body was instantly aroused, then disappointed when he drew back.

With a husky laugh, he murmured, 'Not here, *ma chérie*. Soon, soon.'

Soon? How likely was that, once he heard the news? But after the outcome of her recent tactful inquiry, it felt impossible to break it just then. She'd have to wait until he'd forgotten it.

She hoped the lunch wouldn't take long. What if it went on for ever and she lost the chance to be private with him? Though, was it best to be completely private with him? For this sort of news, maybe it would be as well to have witnesses. A public place would be preferable, perhaps a café.

'You're too quiet,' he observed on the way, paused for some lights. 'What's going on inside that head?'

She met his slanting glance. 'I was just—wondering about your dog.'

'*Comment*?'

'You know. You mentioned a dog.'

He said sharply, 'There is no dog.' Then, flushing a little, he broke into a reluctant laugh. 'Manon—my ex-girlfriend—had a passion to acquire a Russian wolfhound. The Borzoi. You know the one? We discussed it and—decided it would not be practical. I preferred something else.' His hands lifted from the wheel in agitation. 'After the—split, someone in the press heard about it, suggesting that our partnership ended because I would not allow Manon to have the pet she craved. You can imagine, in *France*…I was crucified in the tabloids. You see?' He smiled ruefully.

'Oh.' She swallowed. 'Yes, yes. I see.'

Staring out at the Seine, she kept her hands tightly clasped in her lap. She could see all right.

'What was it you preferred?' she said.

A muscle flickered in his lean cheek. The corner of his mouth made an infinitesimal downward curl that was really quite heartbreakingly attractive. 'Something smaller.'

Tante Laraine lived in the seventh *arrondissement*. Luc pressed a button in what looked like an ordinary wall in the street, and a panel slid open to reveal a security plaque. He dialled in a code and a door opened. Inside, to Shari's surprise, was a beautifully manicured garden with a fountain. A gravelled path led to the side entrance of a gracious old building with the distinctive Parisian mansard roof and dormer windows.

Several children were darting here and there among the

shrubbery, playing a game that required sudden shrieks and bursts of laughter. A couple of them called to Luc, and he waved back.

As she approached the entrance Shari's nerve began to fail. The people inside all thought she was Rémy's fiancée, and here she was, fresh from Luc's bed, pregnant with Luc's child and planning to…what? How could she possibly carry off such a dilemma?

'Luc.' She started to breathe faster than a woman approaching the finish line in the London marathon. 'Do you mind if we don't go here?'

His brows lifted in surprise. '*Pardon?*'

'Could we just go to a café or…' She tried to swallow but she was all out of saliva.

His eyes narrowed on her face. '*Que veux-tu…?*'

'There's something I might have to tell you.'

Some people burst through the doors then, exclaiming when they saw her and Luc. Amidst all the embraces and introductions, her moment was lost, though on the way up in the lift with the others Luc kept looking searchingly at her. He whispered, 'Are you feeling well? Is everything fine?'

'Yep. Fine,' she lied through her lying teeth.

Laraine's apartment was on the top floor below what Shari imagined would be a garret for starving artists and bohemians. When she was ushered inside, though, it seemed possible Laraine kept an army of maids and footmen up there.

The ceilings were extraordinarily high and ornate. As for the furnishings…Shari doubted if the precious pieces had been created any later than the eighteenth century.

Several other family members were present, some Shari recognised from the funeral. Tante Marise. Oncle Georges, whose eyes lit up when he saw her. A couple of younger cousins, Anne-Sophie and Sophie-Louise, with spouses. She'd never remember which Sophie was which. Though warmly welcomed and kissed by all, Shari suddenly felt burningly aware of her casual attire.

A scarf could only go so far to catapult an ordinary Aussie girl into Parisian society. If only she'd done something with her hair. The Sophies looked chic, even in jeans.

Luc glanced at her often, a slight frown in his eyes that made her heart quake. Trust her to choose the exact right moment. She'd alerted him to trouble, and she could see he was speculating.

Contrary to things she'd read, the family seemed happy to converse in English on her behalf, except when they forgot. Luc poured her a sherry and handed her the glass. Feeling his mother's quick glance flick between them, Shari accepted it, taking care not to touch him.

Laraine suspected, Shari saw suddenly. Though how much? Was the Ritz etched into their body language? Or did Laraine have X-ray vision?

Even imagining the impossibility made Shari a tiny bit giddy. With the family all believing she was Rémy's woman, how must it look?

As she allowed her restless glance to wander her nerve jumped. On a side table where some family photos were displayed, the lovely couple blazed out at her. Luc in evening dress, Manon in a beautiful bare-shouldered gown, her hair up, on this occasion honey-blonde. Another of them in relaxed weekend mode with several of the present company. Clearly, Manon had been part of the family.

Excruciatingly out of her comfort zone, Shari answered questions about her journey, Sydney, Emilie and her children, the new twins about to be born, smiling, smiling. Babies, mothers, newborns—all were popular here, apparently.

Shari gazed at her sherry. Would it look suspicious if she didn't drink it? In a limbo of indecision, she held the glass in her hand, untouched.

Not that any of those pregnancy rules would have to apply

to her, necessarily. After all, if she didn't stay pregnant... Why was it so hard to control one's breathing and slow it down?

There was a bit of discussion about Rémy, then the conversation moved on to other things. People appealed to Luc often for his opinion, and when he replied he was always pleasant, measured, amused. Occasionally though he seemed not to hear them. He kept staring at the floor, or at Shari. Then he looked grave and so darkly handsome she felt the twist in her heart that signalled trouble ahead.

As if she didn't have enough.

At a point where the conversation grew loud and lively, Luc strolled over to her and murmured, 'What did you want to talk about?'

'Nothing, nothing. Shh.' She smiled as if everything were as normal as gramma pie while on the inside she was imagining herself growing huge, going to hospital all by herself and coming home to her flat in Paddington, with a... Well, not quite by herself.

The meal was an exquisitely prepared torture.

At first there was foie gras on slivers of toast on her plate. In her strangely disconnected state she couldn't help wondering how many poor geese had died to produce it. Lucky there was some lettuce she could chew on, a few curls of celery.

Sensing Luc's gaze, she was tempted to let their eyes tangle for an instant. His compelled her, questioning, uncertain, and she skittered hers away.

Oh, God. Had he guessed?

'You have made a journey *très, très, vraiment* long, Shari,' Laraine said. 'A pity the occasion is so melancholy.'

The family showed their concern for the grieving fiancée with a series of questions, punctuated by discussions about the food and family concerns Shari wasn't privy to, interrupting themselves and each other so rapidly she found it barely possible to get in a word.

'*Oui, les pois, s'il te plait*. How long were you and Rémy engaged, Shari?'

'Not long. You see—'

'Try some of this, Sophie-Louise. So, Shari…had you planned your wedding soon?'

'No. Well, actually—'

'You are not enjoying your wine, *ma chérie*?' That was Tante Marise, worrying she wasn't partaking of enough sustenance.

Not to be outdone in the hospitality stakes, Laraine quickly asserted her authority. '*Vite, Gilbert, apportes ce Sancerre*. Shari, you have had a terrible ordeal. You must eat to recover your vitality. You will find this chablis is very fine.' She beamed.

It looked beautiful, pale and chill in its crystal glass. Without a doubt, all the food was of the finest, though Shari could barely do more than taste. A rabbit that had scampered across meadows fragrant with thyme before it was murdered. Artichokes dressed in a manner a duke from the Perigord had only recently demanded on his deathbed.

If she didn't drink the wine, would she give offence? Maybe just a sip, though even a sip could damage something very small and fragile. What if she drank it and the poor little face shrivelled up in agony?

Her insides clenched. She put her glass down.

'While you are here you must visit the village where Rémy and Emi grew up,' someone offered.

'I am certain Luc would be happy to take you there and show you everything,' Tante Laraine said warmly. '*Tiens!* I say, we must all go together and picnic in the woods.'

'*Bien sûr*, Shari,' Tante Marise added kindly. 'Rémy would have liked to see you there.'

She guessed they weren't intending to torture her, but with her world now dominated by an embryo—*Luc's*—this constant harking back to Rémy was an agony.

When she wasn't moving her food around the plate or being addressed by someone, Shari rested her gaze on a burnished antique sideboard with lovely pieces of delicately painted china. An exquisite vase holding jonquils, a Chinese bowl, a fragile urn painted with birds and flowers.

Once she disciplined herself to look at Luc firmly, like a normal, non-pregnant person. His eyes locked with hers, alert, guarded, and her heart turned over.

It was during the cheese she lost her cool. Tante Marise said, 'Poor Shari, you must feel you have lost your whole world. *Tsk-tsk-tsk-tsk-tsk.*'

Shari shook her head, ready to deny the charge and explain about Rémy, when Laraine exchanged a meaningful glance with all the others and leaned tenderly towards her.

'Forgive us, Shari. This is a delicate subject, *ma chérie,* but it must be dealt with. We have spoken with Emilie and do not believe Rémy has left any instructions. Are you aware of his thoughts? We must decide how to dispose of his ashes. It is good you are here in France and you are able to participate.'

Appalled, Shari said, 'Oh, look. No, no, please.' She glanced about at their enquiring, sympathetic faces and cast an agonised look at Luc. Then she rose to her feet, the better to breathe.

'Please, you know, you're all being so kind, but I—I really must explain.' She saw Luc's dark brows draw into an alarmed frown, but she carried on regardless. 'The truth is, that while I *was* engaged to Rémy for a while, it was not a—a very happy thing. Our engagement ended several months before he—before the accident.'

A heavy stillness descended on the room. She could hear pigeons cooing on a distant steeple.

'I haven't wanted to mislead you. And truly, I don't want to hurt anyone. I know you all loved him, he was part of your family, but in fact to *me* Rémy wasn't always the most gentle person. He could lose his temper and be really quite—' Just at that moment, her eye fell on the painted urn resting innocently on the bureau.

A horrifying realisation shocked through her. She grasped at her throat. Unable somehow to manage breathing, she felt herself grow unbearably hot, then without warning whirled forward into a bottomless black hole.

Through a misty haze she heard Luc's shocked voice, distant chairs scraping, a babble of consternation. She opened her eyes again immediately, or so it seemed to her. Well, perhaps some time had passed, because she was now horizontal and in another room, her head on a feather soft pillow, a feather-soft blanket tucked around her.

Luc's mother was sitting at her side patting her knee while Luc was standing over her, looking anxious. They didn't notice she was awake because they were deeply involved in an intense, murmured conversation.

Shari couldn't follow it because they were speaking in rapid French. Not all of it, anyway. There was *one* word she picked up. She knew it rather well from years of experience with Emilie.

Enceinte.

She knew the meaning of that, all right. It meant pregnant; with child; having conceived; in the family way; up the duff; in the pudding club; fat. It was Laraine who uttered the fateful word, and when she did Shari saw Luc's face change.

CHAPTER NINE

A STRAINED silence persisted all the way from Tante Laraine's to the Luxembourg Gardens. Luc had hustled Shari so fast out of the family lunch she was breathless. But not nervous. She had no reason to be scared. He was a civilised, non-violent guy, she was an adult woman capable of making her own decisions and defending herself, so this silence wasn't playing on her nerves.

Much.

It was just that, in a small car, when they were physically in such close proximity, she could hear his very breathing. In. Out. In. Out. Or maybe that was the jackhammer in her heart.

Anyway, he parked and took her for a charming stroll through the afternoon shadows, under trees, past grassy banks to a beautiful old rhimey fountain. Most of the people had left or were on their way home. The clowns, a juggler in his harlequin costume. Lovers holding hands. A kid playing with a hoop. Mothers pushing their babies.

Shari wouldn't have minded a few of them hanging around, just in case, but she guessed it was time for them all to repair to their kitchens and prepare the family *cassoulet*.

She concentrated on small things along the way. Water lilies floating on the pond. Jonquils nodding along the garden path, closing their faces now as the shadows lengthened.

They paused by the fountain. Luc faced her. She made her mind go empty, the way she always had when she suspected Rémy was about to strike.

'Do you have something to tell me?' He took her arms in a gentle grasp that might as well have been of steel. There was no escaping this moment of truth.

'Yes.' Not breathing, she met his compelling gaze. 'It's true. I only found out for sure myself this morning. I'm—*we're*—pregnant.'

She braced.

He scrutinised her face for what felt like for ever. Worlds of calculation glinted in his eyes while he evaluated the available data. In a romance novel he would have said *Then we must get married. No question about it.*

'And you are certain?'

That expression on his face. The tinge of doubt. She remembered it well from the night in Sydney. That occasion when he'd asked her how recently she'd seen Rémy. How recently she'd been hot from his cousin's bed.

'Pretty certain,' she said tonelessly. 'I took a pregnancy test this morning. It came up positive. It was what I—expected.'

He didn't lash out, just sat down with her on a nearby bench. But she could see he was in shock. He was blinking fast and there was a pallor under his olive tan, a grave set to his mouth.

'I know what you are wondering,' she said suddenly. 'You're wondering if the child is yours. You're thinking I might be—exploiting this opportunity to foist Rémy's child onto you, and...' Her voice choked up. Tears came into her eyes and she turned her face away.

He took her hand and held it tight. 'Please. I have to ask the question. Is it mine?'

'Yes. *Yours*. Rémy and I hadn't been—together in that way for a long time.'

He searched her face, frowning. Then, dragging his fingers through his hair, he got up and started to pace. 'This—needs serious thought.' He walked, halted, walked again, like a man riven by terrible conflicts. After a few minutes he paused before her. 'What do you want to do? Whatever you choose, will help you.'

Her heart trembled. 'I don't know. I'm still coming to term with it.'

She crossed her fingers. This was the point where the her would take her in his arms and tell her it was the most beauti ful news he'd ever received.

He was silent for a moment. '*Bien sûr*, this is not the idea way for a—a child to be conceived.'

'No.'

'You live in Sydney. I live here. We are separated by a grea distance…'

She closed her eyes. He was a man, she was a woman. Different planets of origin. He hardly needed words to describe the status quo. The separation factors. His hands did the talking for him. Crushed her wayward little hope and put it back in its box.

'You have a career. You are an independent person. Naturally, you value your autonomy.'

'Well, yes…'

He added carefully, 'In France, of course, there are options. I'm not sure how the law exists in Australia…'

She lowered her eyes. 'There are options.'

'Here…I believe it can be as simple as taking a pill.'

She nodded.

He stared at her a while, his eyes glittering, his face tense. 'This is not something—either of us would have planned.'

'No.'

'This—this changes lives. I would not have afflicted you with this problem.'

'Of course not.'

He lowered his lashes, frowning and breathing rather hard. 'So…' A grim tension tautened his lean face. 'Perhaps the obvious thing to do then would be to—take action. *N'est-ce pas?*' His gaze scoured her face, questioning, searching.

The sun went out, or maybe a cloud doused the world. Her limbs suddenly felt chilled. Shivering, she pulled her trench closer. 'Do you mind if I go back to my hotel now? I'm feeling very tired all at once.'

'Of course, of course.' He helped her up, so courteously, so concerned for her comfort, she had the feeling he'd have carried her to the car if she'd requested it.

The drive to the Hôtel du Louvre was even more tense, if possible, than the drive to the Luxembourg Gardens. But it was a different sort of silence. More like Hiroshima, in those minutes after the bomb.

Before all the agony set in.

When they drew up at the hotel, he paused before turning off the ignition, frowning at the hotel entrance. 'Will you be okay here?'

'Of course. It's a lovely hotel. It's very comfortable.'

His frown deepened. 'I—I've never heard anything *against* it. I'm sure it's of a reasonable standard. Clean.'

She nodded.

'And safe? You feel safe here?'

'Yep. Safe.'

'The staff. They are respectful?'

'Very.'

'And the facilities are—*très bon*?'

He was so concerned that despite her internal suffocation she nearly laughed. '*Mais oui. Très, très bon.*'

He got out and strode around to open the door for her, then ushered her in through the revolving door.

He glanced around the small lobby, then faced her, the lines of his face even more taut. When he spoke his words sounded suddenly jerky. 'So—so what will you do now? Will you sleep?'

'Hope so.'

His eyes strayed in the direction of the restaurant, which to her eyes looked warm and charming, with its banquettes bright with red regency stripes. 'What about your dinner? Do you feel you can eat in this place? You hardly ate a bite at lunch.'

'Oh, yes, yes, I did.' She hoped her appetite problems hadn't wounded his feelings. 'The lunch was delicious. Your mother's a wonderful cook. Anyway, I'll—I might have something sent up later.'

He took both of her hands. 'Are you sure this is what you want? To be here now?'

'Where else? I'm not really in the mood for the Ritz.'

He turned sharply away, but not before she saw the flush darken his cheekbones.

She said earnestly, 'Look, you don't need to worry. I just need to think on my own for a bit. I'm sure we both do.'

He kissed her cheeks, then walked to the door, hesitated, then strode back and kissed her on the lips. 'I'll call you later. *D'accord*?'

'Fine.' She nodded. Smiled brightly. 'Thanks.'

Luc drove towards his apartment but not there directly, because he unbelievably took a wrong turn in the streets he'd known since childhood and was forced to backtrack.

Upstairs, he poured whiskey and stood at his window, gazing out over the rooftops, thinking. No, attempting to grasp onto a thought and hold it still.

Of all the women on earth for him to have accidentally impregnated... To think he'd been condemning his cousin's abuse of her, when now he himself had caused her—this.

He hunched as hot shame rocked through him. Shame on Luc Valentin. Shame, shame, shame.

The ironies weren't lost on him.

His ex-lover choosing to have a baby with another man. His new lover—would she even agree to being called that?—reluctantly pregnant with his child.

If it was his.

He tried to think through all the things she'd ever told him about Rémy and the break-up. The time in the boathouse, that moment of exultation when she'd produced the battered package from her purse.

He knew what some guys would think. Had she really just taken the test today? Was it possible she'd come to Paris to snare him, knowing all along she was pregnant? With his cousin's child? For money?

The image of her face, her gentle womanly dignity when he'd questioned her in the Gardens resurfaced. Shamed him afresh. *Scathed* him. *Mon Dieu*, what was he doing? Attempting to escape responsibility?

Needing to escape himself, he locked the apartment behind him, took the creaking old lift down and plunged into the streets.

The lights were glittering all over the city as the evening deepened. Luc strode along in the brisk air, hunched into his jacket, hands in pockets, attempting to clear his mind.

He was a rational guy. In charge of his life. It wasn't such a big thing, after all. People dealt with these little surprises all the time. All the time.

He'd been with Manon when he'd dreamed of them having the child. That time was gone now, destroyed, but he'd learned from it. The male of the species didn't have the right to impose his children on an unwilling female. He could see the justice of that. How some guys still managed to get away with it was a mystery.

An unbidden image of him and Shari with a child flashed through his head, and he banished it. Even if she wanted that, it would never work. Somehow, over the years, disillusionment had accumulated on his heart like so much snow.

Anyway, she'd made it clear she'd never again chance the domestic partnership model. He could well imagine her expression if he suggested anything as archaic as marriage. For all her gentleness and fragility, she could be as sharp as a knife.

She'd laugh in his face. And after her experience with Rémy, who could blame her?

No. In this case the rational decision was the only one. He'd support her through it, every step of the way.

Hopefully what she had to go through wouldn't be too painful. His gut clenched.

The restaurants were filling, people strolling to their entertainments. Tourists, students. He recognised a few of the locals from his neighbourhood. All at once he saw the guy from the *boulangerie*. He was with his wife, laughing with her as they crossed the street.

Luc could see the bulge of something the guy was transporting carefully inside his down jacket, wine bottles perhaps. When they drew nearer and the guy sharpened in focus, Luc saw with a searing pang that the zipper had been pulled down a little to allow a small curly head to peep out.

He turned his face away.

Shari had a good cry in the bath, then got out. Carefully. Her disappointment was cruel, but not a sensible option. Oh, how she hated that word. For a while there she'd imagined she'd glimpsed something more than desire in Luc's dark gaze, more than the amused affection that naturally existed between lovers who'd enjoyed some pleasant intimacy between the sheets.

Maybe if they lived in the same country she'd have a chance with him. But there was no use wanting someone who viewed her as a temporary diversion.

Realising that despite everything she really felt quite genuinely hungry, as if she could actually eat, she dressed in her other jeans and soft blue sweater, adding a pale cream scarf in case, and went down to the restaurant.

The *potage du jour* turned out to be a nourishing vegetable soup. Combined with crusty bread, it was food fit for angels, always supposing angels could eat. Afterwards, feeling fortified enough for anything, she asked the desk manager for an Internet key.

* * *

Luc followed the clerk's directions up to the mezzanine. Through the open office door he saw Shari seated at a desk, her blonde head bent in study of a screen. She was so deeply immersed he knocked twice before she heard him. *'Ça va?'*

She started, glancing up. 'Oh. I thought you were meaning to phone.'

'I needed to see you. Face to face.'

He saw her eyes light up as she searched his face for…what?

Seeing her in the flesh, he ached to touch her, hold her, but he could hardly muscle her out of her chair. Not in her condition.

He stood a little way from her, held back by an invisible line. 'Did you sleep?'

'I tried, but my brain kept going round.'

'Thinking about—*it*?' He grimaced.

She looked wary. 'What else?'

A flicker at the edge of his vision caused him to glance at the computer screen. There was an image of this large glowing ball. A sunburst, or something.

'Tomorrow,' he said firmly. 'We'll see a doctor. Have it confirmed. Take any steps that need to be taken.'

She moistened her lips. 'I'm not sure I'm ready to see a doctor.'

He felt a bolt of surprise. 'But…we must ensure you're safe. I've heard it said that these things are better attended to sooner rather than later.' He noticed a tension in her posture, though she spoke quite casually, her eyes lowered.

'The steps, you mean?'

'Alors, the—the medical support, the—everything.'

He had the sudden sensation his words weren't getting through.

She swivelled her chair a little so she was angled away from him. Her back was straight, her hands clenched on the desk. 'Luc—I'm going home tomorrow.'

The news shocked through him like a blow. Resistance

burned inside his chest. *Mon Dieu*, this… This was surely a
reproach, a lack of confidence in his response as a concerned,
honourable guy.

'*Mais*, Shari, *chérie*…' He made to grasp her arm, then restrained himself when he saw her start back. It wasn't quite a
flinch, but close, and it shocked him. He remembered a couple of other times he'd noticed her brace herself as if expecting physical force, and the dismayed thought occurred to him
that she didn't trust *him*, either. Even after they'd been together. After the things they'd said. Things she'd shared with
him about Rémy.

It wasn't easy with all this churning inside ramping up his
blood pressure, but he made a stern effort to moderate his tone,
slow himself down. Not to sound so—forceful.

He said with difficulty, 'I thought we agreed you would
stay longer.'

'Things were different then. Anyway, I didn't really agree.
I was just—considering it. I don't think we'd enjoy a week at
the Ritz now, somehow.'

Even as she made the comment he could see the resolution firming in her face. That pretty chin could be quite determined. But he had to accept the justice of her words, *bien
sûr*. In this context the Ritz suggestion sounded ludicrous. But
the prospect of her leaving immediately with everything un-
resolved was—wrong.

The screen caught his eye again and he saw it wasn't a
ball, not really. It was a woman's anatomy. Or one part of it,
greatly enlarged.

He summoned the most persuasive smile he was capable of
at that moment. '*Nom de Dieu*, Shari, I'm not implying that we
should just—carry on regardless. But you must agree, something like this requires careful—reflection. And time. Time
to make a reasoned decision.'

'Oh?' She glanced up. 'I thought you'd already decided.'

He spread his hands. '*Zut alors*, we've both decided, *n'est-*

ce pas? Remember what we said in the gardens? We agreed, yes? And we are—aren't we?—on the same page with this*?*'

There was something in her eyes then that made his heart lose the beat, then speed up like a fury.

He hastened to add, 'W-well, as far as one *can* decide at first instinct. We need first to examine all the medical issues. I'm thinking here of your health.'

She lifted her shoulders. 'My health's fine. Anyway, they have the best possible health care in Australia. There's nothing here that I can't have there.'

He said sharply, 'You won't have *me* there.'

His change of tone made her blink. He noticed her stiffen and hold herself so rigidly, anyone would have thought she'd been expecting a blow.

His heart thudded. What did she think? He was like Rémy? After last night? Breathing harshly, he swung away from her towards the door. '*D'accord*, you want to leave. *Très bon*. You must do as you wish. What time is your flight?'

'Noon. I need to be there by ten-thirty.'

'I'll pick you up an hour before.'

'Oh, look. No need to put yourself out. I can take a taxi.'

'*Shari*. Of course I will drive you there.' Shocked, wounded, he stared at her, struggling to interpret the meaning of all this—rejection. Didn't women say they *wanted* guys to support them in this sort of emergency?

She looked so fragile. One of those small, blonde, fragile women one saw at every market. No, he thought at once. Correction. One of those small, blonde, fragile *pregnant* women.

He hesitated for fear of scaring her again. But he couldn't just accept this—dismissal. He needed to remind her of who he was. How they'd been.

He strode back and pulled her up out of the chair, crushed her to him and kissed her. Not a mere milk-and-water kiss like the earlier one in the downstairs lobby, either. This was one of the true ones. Fierce, like his inexpressible heart, and passionate, his hands on her breasts, her gorgeous bottom, the curves that had given him such exquisite pleasure and even now were making him so hard he could have her here and now on this desk.

And he was vindicated. After a stunned second she melted against him and joined him in the torrent of fire, clinging to him with all the fervour and passion he felt himself.

Blessed victory in his hands at last, he broke the kiss. 'Let's go to your room,' he said thickly. 'You don't want to be alone tonight.'

He could see his desire reflected in her eyes, but she dropped her lashes and turned her face away. 'No, look. It's probably best if I *am* alone.'

'*Chérie.*' *Dieu*, his voice was a groan. What was she doing to him? 'I can't—I can't imagine how you will sleep thinking of all these things. You need me to hold you. How else am I to persuade you not to fly away tomorrow?'

She made a grimace. 'That's just the trouble. No. No, honestly.' Evading his hands she backed away, opening a good two metre distance between them. 'I won't be able to think straight if you're here. I owe it to—to myself, to have this night alone. Please, Luc. You have to understand. I *know* Australia. I'll feel more comfortable there, whatever I have to go through. So please…for my sake and for— Well, for *my* sake.'

She virtually *shoved* him through the door. The failed guy, eliminated. The partner in crime, repudiated. The unwanted mate, condemned to a night of sheer and utter hell.

She smiled ruefully, but he saw that in fact she was as inflexible as steel. 'Goodnight.'

Something—*everything* about her seemed different, although maybe it was himself, seeing her through different eyes.

CHAPTER TEN

SHARI had ordered tea and toast to wake up with, and was relieved the early bite made some difference to how she felt. It couldn't have been very beneficial to have been operating on near empty for so much of yesterday. No wonder she'd collapsed at *chez Laraine* and created all that drama.

When she was packed and organised, she rang for her suitcase to be taken down, then waited in the breakfast room where she could watch the street, her trench folded on the banquette beside her. It was still far too early to expect Luc.

From where she sat she could see the waiter across at the Café Palais Royale arranging chairs under his red awning, while next door the patron was sweeping his section of pavement.

Even with her nerves stretched taut as bowstrings she could enjoy the scene, though it was a pleasure tinged with regret. If only she'd had more time to soak up the beauty.

Half her mind was already set on home. Neil had emailed her through the night to announce the safe arrival of the twins. In her rocky state those first photos had been almost too confronting. She supposed drearily if she didn't miscarry it would be comforting to have him and Emilie close at hand to advise her. It wasn't as if she'd be completely alone.

There was a constant ebb and flow of taxis in the square outside, and she had a cowardly impulse to run out and hail one. It wouldn't be fair, but it might spare her some grief. After last night she suspected Luc wasn't altogether satisfied with the prospect of her slipping from his grasp.

Although, maybe now he'd had time to think, he would accept her escape as an easy solution for himself as well. Whatever choice she made, he could go on with his life undisturbed.

She was just considering a tactful way to point this out to him when he walked in, ninety minutes ahead of the appointed time. Her heart lurched. The instant she saw his face she knew this would be no easy departure. It flashed through her mind he must have had an inkling he needed to be quick.

He stood gazing silently down at her, then bent to brush her cheeks with his lips.

He was unshaven, deep lines around his mouth and eyes suggesting he'd experienced a rugged night.

'May I?'

'Of course.' She flushed, ashamed he'd felt he had to ask.

He swung around to signal the waiter. '*Café, s'il vous plaît.*' Then he turned back to her. Scanned her face. She could sense him assessing her mood. 'Shari…'

She braced herself, her heart knocking in her chest.

His dark eyes were arresting in their gravity. 'I can't let you go like this.'

Her nerve plunged. 'But—'

He took her hands and it was as if an electric charge pulsated through her. 'Now I've had time to think, I can guess why you want to run away. I believe I didn't listen to you well enough. Somehow I—didn't hear what you were wanting. *C'est vrai*?'

She looked warily at him. 'Well….you seem—*seemed*—very certain of the way to go.'

'I'm not certain of *anything*.' The words were as raw as if they'd been wrenched from his soul.

'But yesterday you were so keen to—abort at once.'

He flushed deeply. 'Yesterday… *Alors*, I will admit, I felt the need to act.' He opened his hands in appeal. 'Try to understand. My first reaction was to think that for you this is a terrible blow. You are a free, lovely woman—how could I have done this to you? I wanted to deal with it. Spare you as much anxiety as possible.'

He sounded so sincere, she had to believe him.

'I see.' She sat back against the banquette, surveying him. 'I guess I thought you were horrified. Well, naturally, who wouldn't be? Your worst nightmare realised. Me a—a virtual stranger, at the same time embarrassingly connected to your family, and...'

'*Mais non*. How can any of that matter? But I can't deny I do feel—responsible.'

'I know. I do know that.'

Though, to be honest, she hadn't really given his feelings much consideration. She'd assumed he'd made up his mind at once to rid himself of the problem asap. It hadn't really occurred to her he might actually feel perturbed about having potentially changed her life irrevocably.

If she could believe that, it would be a bit of a revelation.

She glanced covertly at him. Apart from Neil, who was a human being, the salt of the earth and the kindliest pushover in the world, the men she'd known hadn't shown much concern for the woman or the child. Obviously they all hadn't been as selfish as Rémy—he'd been in a class of his own—but take her father, for instance. He was no Sir Lancelot. He'd run out on his family *and* on the child support.

Unless he was angling for an Oscar, Luc seemed genuinely distressed. His eyes held a sort of endearing shell-shocked confusion. She slid her hand into his and curled it around his fingers. 'Look, it wasn't just you who made it happen, was it? It was also me. Every step of the way. I wanted to be with you that night. I wanted to experience—you.'

A flame lit his eyes and smouldered there so fiercely she felt scorched. 'And I *you*.'

His glance was so flagrantly sexual at that moment she almost expected him to leap across the table and grab her in full view of the early-morning breakfasters of the Brasserie du Louvre. And, crazed as she was, she'd have let him.

Thoroughly inappropriate.

'And I was the one who produced the faulty you-know-what.'

He winced. 'Don't remind me.'

The waiter set down a coffee pot and cups. Luc slipped the guy a note, then poured the milky coffee.

'So.' He straightened his shoulders and captured her gaze, his eyes serious and compelling. 'I think we must tell each other the truth. What are you thinking, really?'

Aha. Here it came again. The moment of truth.

There were some details too dangerous to share with a man whose first instinct was to pull the chain. Tiny developing eyelids and heartbeats were not likely to sway a guy who was a big player on the Bourse, as Neil had informed her when he was trying to convince her of Luc's importance as a hard-hitting businessman.

She tiptoed as cautiously as a lark upon a leaf.

'Well, er…like you…at first I was so panicked all I could think of were ways of escape. But now…' She strove to keep her face cool and expressionless. She'd learned from Rémy that betraying her schmaltzy interior was a mistake. Squeeze her and she'd squish, and hadn't he just loved to watch that happen? 'The more I—consider, the more I realise I'm not ready to do anything—irrevocable. There's time to decide. A few more weeks, I believe.'

He nodded, slowly and gravely. '*Oui*. I too would like a few more weeks.'

'Really?' She felt a stab of surprise. Why? What was in it for him? Was he having some sort of brainstorm? She tried to read his eyes. 'After all, it is a huge decision.'

He nodded. '*Vraiment* it is huge. So huge we should make it together. Agreed?'

A warning gong tolled deep within her. Togetherness was all very well if they wanted the same thing. But if they didn't…

He watched her face. She could feel the clock ticking for her answer.

'Well…' She reached for her cup. Her hand shook a little and she withdrew it, though not before he'd noticed, to her chagrin. 'Certainly we need a clear picture of where each other stands.'

His eyes glinted, then he frowned down at his coffee. When he looked up he spoke quietly, his tone measured. 'I'm hoping you will agree to stay in France while we consider.'

'What, *here*?' She cast an involuntary look around. 'Oh, no, no. Sorry, I'm not able to manage that. Anyway, I'd prefer to be at home coping with this than in a hotel in a strange country.'

'You misunderstand.' A flush darkened his bristly cheek. 'Not here, *chérie*. With *me*. In my apartment.'

'Oh.'

The apartment, no less.

A sunbeam dangled itself enticingly in the direction of her heart, with hope dancing up and down it in sparkly stars.

She rejected the treacherous thing outright. She'd been sucked in by that sunbeam before. *Big* time. Stars, spangles, the works. This time the risks were far too great. It wasn't just her dreams she had to worry about being flushed down the toilet.

'And you won't be coping alone,' he added, smiling. But she sensed determination behind those eyes. And in the set of his handsome jaw she read assurance. Authority. The man asserting his rights. 'You will have me,' he declared softly.

'Of course.' She beamed him a smile, though her insides were twanging with warnings of caution. 'And I appreciate the offer, I truly do, but I'm probably better to be independent and in charge of my own space, you know?' A wry twitch of his lips only added more momentum to her misgivings. 'I told you. I learned the hard way I'm not cut out for togetherness and the domestic life.'

Maybe he had the misguided belief he was an equal partner in this enterprise, but it wasn't all happening to him, was it? He wasn't incubating little developing networks of nerves and synapses. Arms. Legs.

'Anyway,' she added hastily, 'I haven't brought enough clothes with me for a longer stay, and…I have a book contract I have to fulfil. I need to work. I really do.'

'You can work at my place.' He spread his hands, smiling, insistent. 'Why can't you? And don't worry a thing about your clothes. I'll take care of all that for you. I'm good with clothes.'

This was no recommendation. Rémy had been good with clothes. Good at telling her when she'd got it wrong.

He made a rueful gesture. 'Don't look so mistrustful.' He took her hand and held it between both of his, his dark gaze grave. 'Shari… Please understand. I'm not Rémy. Listen to me. I promise—on my honour I would never do anything to cause you harm.'

His eyes shone with a light that threatened to pierce her total serenity.

With her wobbly heart trembling in its niche all of a sudden, she felt a severe need to loosen her scarf. 'Well, *quel* relief.' She moistened her lips. 'That's…very nice.'

Glancing at her watch, she saw there was still plenty of time, but she wouldn't have minded bolting for the airport right at that very instant. She made to gather her trench. 'Actually, Luc, I don't want to be rude and rush things, but…'

He leaned forward, holding her captive in his dark gaze. 'You're not listening to me, Shari. I'm begging you to stay. I want to support you.'

'Oh, heavens.' Her pulse raced faster than Black Caviar at the Melbourne Cup. Was this the guy in the romance, or was she reading too much into a few words again? 'Why would you want to do that? I can support myself. And I've got Neil. I told you—I'm probably not meant for togetherness.'

'You know why.' His eyes glowed with a serious intensity.

'I want you. I don't want you to disappear to the other side of the world and lose you.'

Oh. Oh, God and the whole set of heavenly virgins. He *looked* so gorgeous, with his dark eyes so intent and sincere…

Like the crazy fool it was, her susceptible heart drank the words in like honey. It faltered in its resolve. Admit it. She was thrilled. All those romantic novels she'd brainwashed herself with from an early age wouldn't be suppressed. In less than an instant she was floating into the realm of candlelit dinners, cuddles by firelight, strolls hand in hand along the banks of the Seine, night after night after glorious night of bliss…

With her lashes fluttering out of control, she said breathlessly, trying not to fixate on his sexy mouth, 'But—you see…I have to be certain. I can't risk…' Like the fool she was, tears chose that moment to swim into her eyes. 'You must understand, I won't be hustled into anything.'

'I do understand. I understand exactly.' He kissed her hand and held it to his chest. 'Feel this? I promise on my heart I won't hustle you into anything you don't enjoy to do.'

She could feel the big muscle pumping under her palm, communicating disgracefully with her clitoris. She was so burningly conscious of the vibrant flesh and sinew beneath his shirt she had to yank her hand back before she did something scandalous.

The temptation to throw herself into his arms and kiss him rapturously down onto the banquette was extreme. But she held back, her bloodstream a torrent of yearning while her last resistance dithered. She'd never so much needed to be rational.

Honestly, maybe she'd be foolish to leave now. Why close off all her options? If he'd truly had a change of heart, this could be for the best, couldn't it? Maybe he would fall in love with her and she'd be the love of his life. Maybe they'd have several children. Two girls and two boys. They'd all go to the Sorbonne and become philosophers, artists and doctors with Médecins Sans Frontières.

'I see. Well. Well, then…' She made herself sound businesslike. Let him know she was in charge of her life and her uterus. 'Perhaps I could consider a—a brief trial. Only a trial, mind. No promises. How about say…a weekend?'

After all, what could he make her do against her will in a weekend?

'A week at least,' he insisted, dark eyes gleaming. 'I will use some vacation time and we can take this chance to—know each other.' That gleam grew so unmistakably sensual she thought she could guess what sort of knowledge he had in mind.

While she knew she mustn't allow herself to be seduced into a maelstrom of mindless passion, her highly susceptible pheromones all thrilled in anticipation.

She said, a little breathlessly, 'But—we need to be practical about this. Are you sure you have enough room? Once I get started on my work, I do tend to spread out a little.'

He threw his head back and laughed, his eyes alight with amusement. 'Don't worry. I can accommodate you no matter how far you spread.'

Well, that was heartening. So was the kiss he locked her in as soon as they were in the car. Well, at any rate it started out as fiery, but then he cooled it to a more tender, controlled sort of kiss, which was all the more arousing because she was so aware of his restraint. By the end she was bursting out of her bra, and aflame between her thighs.

If such a modest kiss could affect her so wildly, surely her decision to stay a while couldn't be all wrong?

On the way to his place, though, she was naturally besieged by second thoughts. How warm would he continue to be when her inner frump broke out? How long could she fake this *soigné* sophistication? Before she knew it she'd be forgetting to wear a scarf and clumping around in Ugg boots.

But he seemed so genuinely chuffed, grinning, chatting, his eyes shining as he pointed out various landmarks to her, she didn't have the heart to pull out right then. And when he opened the door of an apartment on the sixth and topmost floor of a centuries-old building in the *deuxième arrondissement*, and she walked in and saw Paris spreading below through tall windows at every turn, it was a heady moment.

Not quite real, actually.

Luc Valentin wanted her. As she gazed about, blinking at the silk curtains, the ornate mirrors, the rich oriental rugs vying for supremacy on the gleaming wooden floor, the elegant velvet sofas, an actual chandelier in the sitting room, those words kept spinning around and around in her head.

Even with a bun in the oven he wanted her. Could he have noticed how pregnant women *looked* a few months in? Had he realised she wouldn't remain her svelte and lissom self for long?

Maybe he wasn't expecting her to stay pregnant. Her fears all came flooding back, highlighted in red.

'*Bienvenue*,' he said, holding her shoulders, then kissing her lips as she stood in a luxury-induced trance. For such a rich and sophisticated man, he seemed a trifle awkward. 'Please— be as if you are at home.'

'Thank you.' The decor here could put the Ritz to shame. She had a shameful wish it had been a tiny bit more humble. Imposing bureaus and credenzas, while admirable, could be quite lowering. As could walls of peach-coloured silk and a thousand metres of yellow curtains.

But who was she to criticise? She felt strangely tongue-tied, as if the Tardis had set her down in a distant universe.

As his victory glow calmed a little Luc looked closely at her. She stood apparently rooted midway between the sitting room and the entrance, gazing about. He felt a pang of uncertainty. Somehow here she seemed smaller and more vulnerable, as if she'd shrunk back into herself.

'Are you feeling well?' he said. 'Can I offer you something? Coffee?' With a leap of inspiration he came up with his furthest reach of hospitality to date. 'Tea?'

Not that he could guarantee there would be any.

'Not just now, thanks.'

He felt a strong and manly urge to seal his triumphant possession of her on the nearest available surface, but he sensed the timing would be wrong. And with her condition, he might have to check first about the safety issue.

He made a mental note to conduct some research at the earliest opportunity.

'Perhaps you would like to—unpack?'

She cast him a hesitant glance. He had the sinking feeling she was about to refuse, but she only said, 'Your apartment is very nice. Are all of these family heirlooms?'

'Somebody's, perhaps. Not my family's.'

'Oh. I—I was reminded a bit of your mother's. I thought she might have…' she waved her hand '…you know, contributed when you moved out of home.'

Amusement at the thought of Maman parting with her precious things to accommodate Manon's ambitions made Luc smile. Then he saw Shari flush and felt an instant rush of remorse. What a clumsy idiot, embarrassing her when she was clearly feeling shy.

'Nothing like that,' he hastened to assure her. He flicked a glance about at the place. It was so long since he'd really looked at it, he'd forgotten how appalled he was initially by all the yellow. A man could get used to anything. But could a woman? An *Australian* woman?

'My ex-girlfriend is—er *was* a—a… What do you call—a professional designer. This was how she—liked things.'

Nom de Dieu. Horror gripped him by the balls. Had he really brought up Manon in the first minute? *Zut*, why was it that with Shari Lacey he was as inept as an adolescent?

'Come,' he said hurriedly. 'I'll show you everything.' He reached for her suitcase.

Feeling gauche, Shari followed. Now she could see the hand of a designer everywhere she looked. The matching armchairs by the fireplace. Those two chairs she glimpsed facing each other across that small perfect table in the kitchen. All the yellows blending, complementing each other.

Maybe it was her imagination, but the sum effect was of more than mere luxury. It was also somehow—intimate. As if two minds entwined as one occupied this retreat from the world.

She followed him along a silk-lined hall to some double doors.

'*La chambre à coucher.*' He opened them with an offhand gesture.

Shari drew in a breath. Wow. What a chamber. Spacious, panelled in more peach silk, it was a decorator's dream, rich with fabrics and plushness.

At Luc's urging she ventured in a few steps, and felt an immediate sense of having intruded. Naturally, she supposed, the space had a deeply personal ambience. She let her gaze dwell on the three sets of windows with long silk lemon curtains tied back with sashes. She could see charming little balconies outside.

She tried not to stare at the most dominant piece in the room, but it screamed at her. Wherever she looked, Luc and Manon's bed bore down upon her with its handsome bedhead, the matching lamps on either side. Their pillows. Their sumptuous counterpane.

Feeling Luc's narrow appraisal, Shari turned away, wondering if it was striking him how awkwardly she fitted here in his private space. *Their* space.

Directly facing the bed and above the fireplace was a modern erotic painting of lovers locked in the primal embrace. Following her gaze, Luc started, blinking at it, then stepped forward and snatched it down. Sliding it to the floor, he turned it to the wall.

He gave a jerky, dismissive wave. 'A poor choice. I've always been meaning to dispose of it.'

He turned away to open another set of doors that led into

a smaller chamber of lamps and mirrors, with large wardrobe cupboards lining one wall, a sumptuous chaise longue and a pretty bathroom beyond.

'*Le boudoir*.' He placed her suitcase inside. 'For—the woman. I have my own dressing room next door, as you see.'

Shari's gaze settled on the woman's dressing table. It was delicate-looking, with wavy lines, a beautiful winged mirror and a matching chair covered in rose and lemon patterned silk. Some highly polished perfume bottles sparkled before the mirror, while a tortoiseshell hairbrush still lay in wait for its rightful owner. Shari could almost see the chic and elegant woman seated there, completing her *toilette*.

Luc hastily strode forward and swept the surface bare, dropping the items into a silk-covered waste bin. 'The maid should have attended to this. I'm extremely sorry.' He looked so stern Shari hoped the maid wouldn't have to face him soon. He opened a closet door, then with a muttered curse closed it again quickly before she could see inside.

The air prickled with discomfort. Shari hardly knew what to say. 'It's all—gorgeous.' She gestured around at the exquisite room. 'My suitcase is ruining the effect.'

He closed his eyes. 'Not at all. Your suitcase is the only reality in a—a ridiculous fantasy. She—Manon—liked to feel like a courtesan of the First Empire.' He gave a terse laugh, then backed out of there rather quickly. 'And ah…as you see… all—all of our balconies are very small, I regret to say.' He gave a swift smile. 'Not like in Australia.'

'Nothing is like in Australia.'

He stared at her for a strained second, then said tensely, 'There is another bedroom you might prefer until we prepare this one properly. Come and see.'

He slipped his arm around her and kissed her ear. Pulled her against him and buried his face in her hair. 'Ah…the scent of you. Shari…' he breathed. 'Relax. Don't be upset by small things. Don't worry. I will…' He kissed her and she felt the vibrancy of his hard body pressed against hers, but she disentangled herself.

It didn't feel right kissing him in there.

The guest room was charming, though not in the same class of opulence. While there was no boudoir attached, Shari thought the capacious armoir more than sufficient for her belongings. As well there was a chest of drawers and a small bathroom.

'This'll be fine,' she said, smiling. 'I'm probably not the courtesan type.'

With a flush darkening his tan, he took her arms. 'Shari,' he said stiffly. 'Please accept my apologies. I should have thought before I— I don't spend any time here now, so I never look at the rooms. I can't imagine why I haven't thought of changing things. It's purely an oversight.'

'It's okay, really. It's not as if you had any advance warning. I'm fine. Don't worry.'

'It won't be so terrible in here for an hour or two, *n'est-ce pas*? I believe the bed is soft. Would you like to unpack?' He stared hungrily from her to the bed. 'Or—to rest?' His eyes grew searingly wolfish.

'I wouldn't mind going for a walk, actually.' She definitely needed a breather. Time out to reflect. 'Stretch my legs.'

He looked worried, but then he shrugged. '*D'accord.*'

It was a relief to be out in the air. Shari sensed Luc feeling more relaxed too. Conversation was easier without the ghostly presence of his ex. And there was so much to see around her, every boulevard and every narrow alluring lane, she tried not to dwell on the glimpse she might or might not have caught into the inner guy.

Did a man keep his old lover's belongings intact simply because he forgot to remove them? Or because he couldn't bear to part with them?

Or was the maid entirely to blame? Could she have been a Mrs Danvers, by any chance?

Anyway, this wasn't a Gothic novel and she was probably reading too much into a small thing. And it was pleasant strolling with a gorgeous guy who took her hand from time to time and seemed to regard her as a fragile vessel.

It was an impression she was eager not to correct before she'd at least had a good wallow in it. Just supposing she stayed the whole week. It was comforting to remember she still had options.

Although she'd managed by the skin of her teeth to postpone her flight home for another week, the day of departure could be changed again, depending on available seats. Nothing was set in concrete.

It wasn't as if she were dreaming of moving in. But a week's holiday with him could be very acceptable. *Could* be. Though he wasn't just talking a week, was he? Underneath it all, she sensed he wasn't kidding about wanting her to stay longer.

She chewed her lip.

Even if he was still in love with Manon, what difference did it make? Did a woman need to be loved by the father of her child? She could still have a good time with him, couldn't she?

Anyway, what was she angsting over? The elegant woman was long gone.

Surely.

She gave Luc's bicep a friendly squeeze through the cashmere. Finding it so satisfyingly hard she couldn't even make a dent, she grinned. 'How I love a hard man. What do you do in the evenings, monsieur?'

He shrugged. 'Until this moment I—work, or I attend dinner meetings, *soirées*. *D'Avion* is quite important to the French economy, so sometimes I'm invited to attend receptions with people in the government. Concerts, the opera, the cinema… What does anyone do?'

She had visions of him in evening dress, whirling around the sophisticated Parisian social scene. No doubt since he didn't have Manon to accompany him he'd found other women to escort. Maybe he held a different beauty in his arms every night of the week.

Though not in his apartment, clearly.

'Don't you ever feel like a night in?'

'I think I might feel like one tonight.' Though he spoke gravely, his eyes gleamed and she felt a tingle of excitement. It could be all right. If she gave it a chance.

At least he was patient to walk with. He didn't seem to mind or try to chivvy her along when she stopped to gaze into shop windows. Even when she ventured inside for a closer look he hung around outside, talking on his mobile. Probably chatting to government ministers or giving instructions to people in his office. Or maybe he was warning his girlfriends not to expect him for a night or two.

After a few fascinating blocks they turned into the Rue Montorgueil, which was a market crowded with shoppers patronising the dozens of cafés and patisseries, food and wine shops.

Charmed to her socks, she forgot all her misgivings and oohed and ahhed like a tourist. The rue was a Monet come to life.

'Do you cook?' he enquired, pausing by a cheese emporium.

'Not in France. Do you?'

He laughed at her quick response. 'I don't have to. I have a hundred restaurants on my doorstep. But for you I'll turn the leaf.'

He purchased several varieties of cheese, some sausage slices, a crusty loaf and fruit, olives and some salad vegetables from a market stall brimming with fresh produce. Then, apparently exhausted by such heavy domestic activity, he suggested lunch, steering her towards a café with red geraniums spilling from planters on its window ledges.

Relieved not to be returning to the apartment straight away, Shari sank down gratefully at the table the waiter had directed them to, while Luc piled his purchases on an empty chair. So much had happened in the last twenty-four hours she felt close to a reality overload.

She gave her order, then listened while Luc discussed his choice with the waiter. When the guy bustled away, Luc excused himself and drew out his phone.

'Are they needing you at your office?'

'Not at all. I'm conducting some research.'

After a while she said gingerly, 'Did… Was Manon a good cook?'

He kept his eyes lowered to the phone. 'She could barely cook an egg.'

It was pretty clear what he'd seen in the Parisian paragon. 'Did you and she dine out every night?'

He frowned. 'Most nights. Though our work commitments often meant not with each other.'

'When did you ever talk?'

He said drily, 'There was nothing to talk about.'

She studied him covertly. His face was as close to expressionless as a frowning man could achieve.

'I can see your point about keeping a large dog in your beautiful apartment.' She filled her water glass and took a sip.

He looked up sharply then, his eyes so cool she nearly jumped back in her chair. 'Have you noticed we have had nearly two full days now without rain?'

'Sorry.' She winced. 'Too forward?'

He took up his phone to deal with an incoming text. 'There are so many other things worth discussing.'

The waiter arrived with their meals. Shari welcomed the diversion. She felt a bit shaken, actually. She certainly hadn't intended to strike any major nerves.

She murmured to the waiter, 'Could you please bring my salad now?'

The waiter's brows elevated. 'Now? Both? At the one time?'

'*Oui, s'il vous plaît.*'

He threw up his hands, then hurried away to comply, shaking his head at her unfathomable foreignness.

Shari contemplated her *croque Mediterranéen*, conscious of a jagged sensation. Though Luc continued courteous, there was something forbidding in his expression. She accepted it was her own fault. She'd pushed the boundaries and now he'd vanished behind a steel barrier.

All at once she felt adrift in an arctic sea. The Luc who had begged her to stay and kissed her in the car had become a stranger. She'd never been good at coping with angry people. If he didn't smile soon she didn't know what to do. 'Look, I—I apologise if I intruded. I know it can take a long time to forget.'

He looked up at her, his dark eyes glinting and alert. 'That depends on what there is to forget.'

'Of course, of course. Sorry. What do I know?'

She tasted her salad. Oh, *God*. Divine. The dressing was to die for. Exactly what she'd anticipated.

It was just as Rémy had declared. Every French person expected—*demanded*— their salad be dressed with just such a superb vinaigrette. She'd never managed to get it exactly right for him. What was she doing here? How could she possibly contemplate a whole week with another Frenchman? What did she know of Luc anyway? He dined with people in the government. He attended soirées. He was in love with a beautiful woman she could never compete with.

Glancing about her, she had the panicked realisation she'd never make it here. She just didn't fit. In his apartment. In his life. She started as Luc's voice cut through her musings.

'You're not losing your nerve?'

She glanced up guiltily. Was she so transparent? But what was there to say? She should have boarded that plane and be headed for the Antipodes right now.

His dark eyes searched hers, questioning, bemused. 'Seriously, Shari... Because of a few bottles?'

'No, no. It's—a matter of common sense. Of—of—self-preservation.'

He stared at her, shaking his head, then, leaning forward, said earnestly, 'It's a matter of trust, *chérie*. And of courage. The risk is no greater for you than it is for me.'

'But yes it *is*. You are safe and secure in your country, your culture, while *I* am…'

He grabbed her knife hand to stop its flailing. 'Do you think I haven't considered all of this? But what do *I* know of *you*? I've known you five minutes and you have a child inside you—my child, so you *say*—and unless I'm a perfect saint of a guy you are threatening to run away with it either to abort it without my knowledge or let it be born without me.'

Some of those words sliced her like knives. All her hopeful instincts, fragile as they'd been, shrivelled. She laid down her knife and fork, breathing hard, and met his blazing eyes.

'Yep. That's about the size of it.'

She got up and walked out. Once in the street, she ran.

CHAPTER ELEVEN

IT WAS as well Luc's strides were longer than Shari's because she could run amazingly fast for a pregnant person.

When had a woman been more difficult to pin down? It was absurd how hard this—this *conquest* was proving. An unwelcome flash of déjà vu rocked through him just then and nearly stopped him in his tracks.

Zut, it was his recurring nightmare. The last time he tried to pin down a woman she'd left him. Abandoned her home and her world.

Surely this wasn't the same though. It was in no way the same.

Dodging people and traffic, he cursed himself fiercely for the fiasco of the day. Everything had gone wrong. He'd *known* Shari was in a volatile frame of mind. Of course she was, in her condition. Why hadn't he noticed the state of the apartment? This was no way to bring a woman home.

But why couldn't women understand that forcing a man into this ridiculous pursuit procedure only roused him to more lust? The more he ran, the more his blood seethed in his veins with a single red-hot intent.

As if he hadn't done enough to her already, he was conscious of a primitive need to catch her and take her down. On the pavement. On the street. Or at least rush her to his bed and plunge himself into her until she surrendered herself to him in screaming ecstasy.

At the same time he felt constrained by an opposing instinct to handle her as if she were made of the most delicate porcelain. The woman had him tied up in knots.

His heart muscle was working overtime by the time he caught up with her. When he saw how her eyes hardened to see him, his gut clenched. The impulse to grab her and kiss her, plunge his tongue into her mouth until her knees buckled was overwhelming, but he restricted himself to gently touching her arm.

'Shari. Please, will you calm down?'

She slowed her pace to a very fast walk, her face set against him.

'What are you doing? Where are you running?' He knew his voice sounded too harsh, courtesy of his pounding blood pressure. '*Should* you be running?'

'I'm going back…'

'*Mais pourquoi*? *Bien sûr, je suis un bâtard, Shari, mais j'ai…*' In the stress of the moment he didn't hear everything she'd said, then realised it was the apartment she was returning to. For the moment, anyway.

'…my things.'

'But why?' He'd just launched into an emphatic and just defence of his behaviour when a series of shouts that had been in the corner of his ear all along finally captured his attention. Turning, he recognised Louis, the waiter from the café, jogging along behind him with the shopping bags.

With emotion running higher than the Eiffel, he was hardly in the mood to smile, but there might have something comical in the scene. The red-faced guy puffing to catch up with them acted as a circuit breaker. He was obliged to stop and was relieved to see that at least Shari paused too, looking on with a polite smile while he showered Louis with thanks and euros.

With passions under tighter controls, they resumed walking, Luc racking his brains for something he could say to minimise the damage and manoeuvre events into a situation he could control.

'Perhaps I need to explain,' he said, as calmly as he was able with his adrenaline ready to burst the levees. 'What I said in the café was not intended the way it may have sounded. I didn't mean you to think I don't accept your word.'

'No?' She cast him the sort of glance usually reserved for snakes.

He felt stirred to defend himself. '*Chérie*. What I said burst from my heart in the heat of the moment.'

'Exactly.'

'*Mais non*. You misunderstand. I was trying to demonstrate how we must trust each other.' He waved the salad bag. '*Vraiment*, we are in similar boats, you and I.'

'You think?' She gave a hollow laugh. 'I doubt if you'd like the view from this canoe, *monsieur*.'

Anyone would have thought he was a selfish animal, without a vestige of humanity. But since they were approaching his building, he restrained his impassioned defence.

'*Mademoiselle*,' he said with restrained dignity, 'we are nearly there. Let us not argue before *Madame la concierge*.'

She froze him with a glance.

It was challenging to know whether she was so complicated because she was a woman or because she was an Australian. Or was it purely the result of her being pregnant? Of course, he had to remember she was used to being with a violent psychopath.

She needed to learn there were guys in the world who knew the meaning of civility, even if they occasionally overlooked a few minor details in the matter of their surroundings.

He turned away from her to greet the concierge. '*Madame. Comment ça va*?'

He listened with greater attention than usual to the latest about the old woman's grandson, her daughter-in-law, and her arthritic cousin in Nantes. Only when the *vieille* was threatening to open up her concerns about her entire extended family did he deal with the issue of addressing the boxes he'd instructed the maid to leave with her. As well, he provided Madame with enough euros to cover the cost of postage, along with a generous contribution towards her retirement fund.

After that burst of friendly conversation, the journey up to the apartment was tense, as if one false word could detonate an explosion. He kept to his side of the lift, Shari to hers.

Shari held herself taut, resisting the current of sexual electricity rampant in the confined space.

Every so often his hot angry glance flickered over her, causing her to burn with indignation. While she'd at last intuited that he wasn't likely to slam her with his fist, it was pretty clear there were other desires percolating through his handsome head.

As if.

Did men ever think of anything else but sex?

He looked as sulky as a boy, but what right did *he* have to be upset? It was as clear as a bell what she had to do.

In the apartment, while he shoved his purchases into the fridge willy nilly, she said politely, 'Would you mind if I used a laptop?'

'*Certainement.*' He crammed the door shut on the foodstuffs. Then with the most elaborate courtesy he showed her into his office and switched on his computer. He leaned down to type in a password. 'If you are wishing to send an email...'

'I'm booking a flight.'

His handsome face stiffened. 'I see. Then in that case...'

He hit the Internet connection and stood back, with a flourish of his hand indicating she should use his office chair.

She sat down and clicked to the site. She could feel his hand on the chair, his fingers brushing against her hair. 'Are you intending to watch over my shoulder?'

He said evenly, 'I'm not watching. I am remaining here to offer my moral support.'

'Just a bit late,' she murmured.

She regretted saying that, actually. Glancing up, she caught an accidental glimpse of his reflection in a mirror that hung outside in the hall.

He'd moved back to glower against the filing cabinet, his arms folded across his chest, dark eyes smouldering, his brow like a storm cloud. Every line of his lean body looked furious. But what did *he* have to feel so raw about? She was the one In Trouble.

Considering he didn't want to be burdened with another man's offspring, he was taking her decision to leave hard. She supposed it must be a macho thing. The caveman wanted to feel in control of the cavewoman, regardless of whose embryo she was incubating.

She typed in her credentials, then scrolled through the flight times.

Disappointingly, all remaining flights for the day had been filled. Conscious of Luc's acute gaze trained on the screen, she tried for tomorrow's with the same result. Incredulously she tried the following day's flights, and the day's after.

No good. She realised despairingly that, unless she wanted to sacrifice the ticket Neil had purchased for her and try another airline, she was stuck for the whole week.

She even tried other airlines, knowing she'd never really waste Neil's generous gift. Then, to underline her terrible luck, the website she was struggling with froze.

Only just resisting smashing something and bursting into tears, she stood up abruptly and turned towards the door. 'This is a waste of time. I'll go back to the Louvre instead.'

'Why?' he said sharply. 'Because I stated what is true between us? *Ecoute.*' He grabbed her and turned her to face him. His dark eyes were cool and stern. 'I'm not a perfect guy, Shari, but I am attempting to be—to *do* what is the right thing. I understand you were upset today with the perfumes, the apartment, but—most of that is fixed now. I was tactless to say what I said in the café, perhaps, but what do you expect?' He flung up his hands. '*Zut*, we are from opposite ends of the earth. And, yes, yes, I know. *You* are a woman, *I* am an idiot. I will offend you—you will offend *me*, perhaps—many, many times, but… *Nom de Dieu*. This talking with you is like walking on eggs.'

She hissed in a breath through her teeth. Her overstressed heart smarted. But while strongly in need of sinking down in a heap and weeping the hot, bitter tears of the chastised damsel, somehow she managed to resist caving in to that final humiliation.

'In case it has escaped your notice,' she said stiffly, the merest tremor in her voice, 'there are some things that do upset the average woman.'

'I've heard. And I'm guilty of all of them.' He flung up his hands, his sexy lips crushing each other in their vehemence.

'No.' She made a desperate bid to gather her serenity about her. 'Maybe you're right. I may have been a bit tense today. Maybe I've been unfair, but at least *try* to extend the limits of your male imagination. I have something—some*one* growing in here.' Raking his lithe, angular, non-pregnant form with her eyes, she clutched her stomach region. 'It's hard to be charming and elegant when little eyes and ears are suddenly developing inside you. How do you think you'd cope with it, *monsieur*?'

His eyes glinted. 'I think I can imagine it. I have seen *Alien,* the movie. But surely the ears don't start to develop for another week or two?'

'What?' Jolted, she ignored his silky Gallic sarcasm to stare bemusedly at him. 'Where'd you get that?'

A rather diffident expression crossed his face. Then his sensuous mouth relaxed and he looked less angry. Less sulky. His dark lashes flicked down as if he was suddenly feeling confident. Smug, even.

He lifted his shoulders with elegant nonchalance.

'Last night, naturally, I was—working. As a pure accident or some strange prompting of fate I happened to stumble across a website that illuminated the—what do you say?—prenatal stages. It seems it is a long process, this development of the senses.' While she goggled, his hands made an earnest demonstration of her abdomen growing to the size of a football field. '*En fait*, while some hearing will certainly be possible soon, I believe the entire auditory channels aren't properly established until some time well after the baby's birth. Eighteen months or so. It is still a very sensitive time in a child's brain.'

'Oh.' She mouthed the word, actually. For though she parted her lips, no sound would come out.

Shock, of course. She'd imagined he'd used both the b word and the ch word, when even in her deepest womanly recesses she hadn't permitted *herself* to think those frightening terms.

He placed his hand gently over her womb. 'We'll have to be very careful.'

As she stared down at that lean, tanned hand a sexual lightning bolt sizzled along her veins. Her mildly emotional state intensified a thousandfold, only it was with a more positive emotion, a more *physical* emotion, if such a thing could exist.

It certainly existed right then. Her devastated heart opened to him, while the rest of her being hotted up like crazy.

'*Well*. I had no idea you…I'm surprised,' she breathed. 'I didn't *expect* you to… Well, to be interested.'

'I am interested.'

'I thought you were deeply horrified by—the situation.'

'I am thirty-six years old, Shari. An unexpected child—could be a beautiful gift.'

Oh, God. Her thrilled heart shook like an alder. 'Well, you know…I'm so sorry about everything.' Her eyes misted and her voice choked a little. 'I know I've been too difficult. And too emotional. And I am a terrible frump.'

'No, you haven't. And you are not.' His deep voice thickened. His hands travelled up her arms to her shoulders, where it was a short and entirely natural distance to her breasts. 'I've behaved like *un imbécile*. Here you are feeling strange and unnatural and I have to behave like a… You're—an angel. You're perfect. So beautiful, so feminine. I want to…'

What he wanted to do he never quite had the chance to say, because even as her heart thrilled with more incredulous trembly emotion he started to kiss her face and eyes and throat. But he did murmur, 'I don't want us to be angry, *chérie*,' and a lot of passionate and tender-sounding things in French—at the same time as sliding his hands under her top and unfastening her bra.

His lips found hers. She was so glad she hadn't fled home with her tail between her legs. A man who could kiss like this deserved every chance to prove himself. While his tongue touched the insides of her mouth with fire and ignited her blood, he held her breasts in his hands and gently pinched her wildly responsive nipples.

She made no attempt to resist the sexual maelstrom. With desire blazing in every corner of her being she burned like a beacon, pushing up his black sweater the better to explore his gorgeous chest and rouse him to the same flaming lust consuming her.

She didn't even have to try. The heat of his satin skin seared her palms, while one lick of his nipples had a dynamite effect. The rigid length straining against his jeans testified to that.

He stopped her hands from travelling too far, though still kissing her, he slipped *his* hand down inside her jeans. At the first delicious stroke of his fingers through the fabric of her pants she was moist, urgent to take him inside.

She clung to him, wrapping her legs around him as he carried her. Somehow they divested themselves of their clothes without completely separating for more than a second here, a moment there.

He pushed her onto the bed with his powerful body, and she surrendered, locking her ankles around him. His magnificent penis, hot, hard and virile, teased the yearning entrance of her sex deliciously.

Thrilling, she held her breath.

His dark eyes burned fiercely into hers. 'Are you certain we should? Will it be too rough? Am I too *grand*?'

She held back a laugh. 'Never too *grand*, monsieur. And I'm hoping for some rough.'

His eyes gleamed, then he thrust inside her with devastating conviction. The fantastic friction turbo-charged her excitement to such a violent pitch of ecstatic passion, she exploded into climax faster than was decent.

It was a long afternoon. After a time, though time was hazy, she pushed Luc onto his back and said, smiling, 'Now then, lover. I'll try not to be too rough.'

Straddling his narrow hips with sinful intent, she slid onto him and rode him until his dark impassioned eyes lost focus and the world dissolved in bliss.

CHAPTER TWELVE

IN THE heat of the moment, Shari hadn't paid a great deal of attention to the *chambre à coucher* to which she was being transported. But there came a time when her eyes opened wide.

The room was still a yellow fantasia, but the empty space above the fireplace was now occupied by an exquisite rococo painting of some gentlemen with ladies—fully clothed—in voluminous dresses, lounging under the spreading boughs of a tree.

She studied it thoughtfully. She felt pretty sure she'd seen it somewhere before. It was too far away for her to take a squiz at the artist's name, but she thought she'd wait until she was alone before investigating.

An expedition to the boudoir revealed that all evidence of any female occupation prior to her own had been obliterated. *Her* perfume bottle now graced the dressing table, and her clothes, meagre as they were, were hanging in the wardrobe. Her shampoo bottles imbued the bathroom with a personality she could feel at home with.

Returning to Luc's arms, she snuggled against his chest. His bristly jaw brushed her forehead. 'I love that picture.'

'Mmm.' His voice was a contented growl. 'Me too.'

She spun a whorl of chest hair around her finger. 'Since you've got a maid to leap to your every command, I'm thinking now I might stay the whole week.'

He sighed. 'Suppose I hire a *chef*? Then you will stay even longer.' When she failed to reply, he gazed down at her. 'Be my lover…'

Well. This came pretty close to sounding like a commitment, of sorts. Her heart shivered with joyful doubt and excitement. 'You do know I'm about to get really enormous?'

'Every man in Paris will envy me.'

She wrinkled her nose. 'Are you sure? Wait till I tell Neil.' Then meeting his amused, tender gaze, she said, 'This isn't just because I'm pregnant and you've been harbouring some weird sicko fantasy about pregnant women?'

He laughed heartily, then tenderly tweaked her hair. 'It's because you are you.' His eyes grew serious. 'Beautiful, unique you.'

He kissed her then, with such passionate ardour she believed him. Believed every word.

And knew she was in love. All at once Paris was heaven. The sun came out, the trees glowed greenly and the flowers in the gardens all opened their beauteous faces. She strolled along the banks of the Seine with her lover, argued with him, teased and drank coffee with him in cafés on the Left Bank. She visited Notre Dame de Paris with him and was awed.

She prevailed on him to take her to all the tourist hangouts, and he obliged without protest, regaling her with a dizzying lunch at the top of the Eiffel Tower, hours and hours of pictures in galleries all over Paris, and dinners in restaurants where the waiters could run up steep flights of stairs balancing steaming trays aloft on one hand.

It was too early to share her news with the world, so she was cagey even with Emilie and Neil. 'I've decided to stay on for a week or two,' she told them in her email. 'Luc has come to my rescue and he's letting me stay at his place for some of the time.'

At his place. Not *with* him. She hoped they got the distinction, though, red-eyed and sleepless from attending to the latest set of twins all night through, they were hardly likely to notice anything.

She included a few pics of Disneyland, some of them strolling in Montmartre, and one rare one she just couldn't resist of Luc laughing while getting drenched in a downpour of rain.

When the possibilities of varying her limited wardrobe reached saturation point, Luc took her to a boutique in the Rue Cambon, near the Ritz, that blessed venue, and some others in the Rue du Faubourg St Honoré. She tried on dozens of things, and he wanted to buy her most of them, but she accepted one lovely pale green dress to wear for daytime occasions and two for evening—one a simple, stunning black, the other a pale silvery cream.

She would never have been able to afford them herself, though she kept a tally of the cost so she could pay him back when her first truly massive royalty cheque arrived, just supposing one ever did. And she allowed the generous guy to give her some pearls and matching earrings as an outright gift.

She insisted on buying herself the shoes though, and, with the weather warming, trawled the Galleries Lafayette for some cooler things for casual wear. She couldn't imagine how large she might be in a few months' time, but there was the rest of spring and a certain amount of summer to live through first.

In her third week in Paris she was booked for her first prenatal visit. A private clinic had been recommended to Luc by a friend in the medical profession. It was the finest in Paris, the friend had assured Luc; reputed to be the most cutting edge in Europe.

The clinic was in the sixteenth *arrondissement*, across the river from Tante Laraine's, though not far as the crow flew. In fact, after their big appointment, as Luc casually informed Shari over his breakfast croissant, his mother had suggested they join her for lunch.

'Oh, have you *told* her?' Shari said quickly.

'Only that you're still in Paris,' he said soothingly, the shimmer in his eyes informing her he was perfectly alive to her alarm on the mother front.

The consultation alone was enough for Shari to worry about, without mothers—and *such* mothers—thrown in.

She put her anxieties aside and focused all her energies on preparing her questions for the doctor. Luc seemed as eager and excited as she was herself, an energy in his stride and a gleam in his eyes that melted her heart whenever he glanced at her.

Finally they were ushered into the consulting room and spent an arduous and exciting hour with the obstetrician, who was a pleasant and efficient Frenchwoman.

There was an endless list of questions for each of them to answer in regard to their family health histories, forms to fill out and government stuff to take care of.

Her official status in France was one of the items at issue.

'My visa is good for another two months,' Shari explained. 'It will have to be extended, of course.' She glanced at Luc. 'Will that be a problem, do you think?'

He looked thoughtful, then shrugged. 'Somehow we will deal with it.'

Then it was time for her examination. Luc didn't appear to enjoy the pelvic part. Not that he was able to see much from where he was standing, wearing an expression of extreme pain.

His face lightened with relief when the doctor finally peeled off her gloves and pronounced her healthy, and, as far as she could ascertain, *l'enfant* progessing normally.

L'enfant. Shari's heart skipped a beat.

And that was just the beginning. By the time the doctor had informed them of the sort of changes to expect along the way, the routine tests and ultrasounds Shari would undergo and her dietary requirements, her head was spinning.

'We will book your ultrasound for twelve weeks. Then we can measure your baby, check for certain of the possible abnormalities, the heart, et cetera. If we have any concerns at that point there's a remote possibility we might schedule you for an amniocentesis test.'

'I've read about that.' Shari couldn't help wincing. 'Is that where they insert a needle into your womb?'

For Luc's benefit, the doctor explained the procedure and its purposes fully.

'It is not routine these days to take this test. Only if there are particular concerns, and of course even then it is your own choice whether or not you have it,' the doctor continued. She produced a booklet that described the whole thing in detail.

Luc looked worried. 'But it sounds… How safe could it be?' He glanced from Shari to the doctor.

'*Bien sûr*, any intervention carries a risk, *monsieur*,' the doctor replied. She indicated the booklet with all the different tests profiled. 'The risk is there, but it is quite small. The statistics are tabled in here. I advise you to study everything carefully.' While encouraging, her cool professional smile revealed no clue of her own feelings on any matter.

Out in the street, floating, dancing, pirouetting the few blocks to where they'd left the car, while Luc was absorbed in some deep Gallic thinking, Shari was infected with an Australian need to babble.

'It's beginning to feel very real.' She fanned herself with pamphlets. 'I'm actually creating a new person. I'm turning into a mother before your very eyes. *Me*. Who would've thought?'

Luc roused himself from his reverie and slipped his arm around her. 'It isn't so impossible to imagine.'

'You think? Have you imagined it? What about you? Do you see yourself as a papa?'

He shrugged nonchalantly, straightened his shoulders and flexed a thousand or so muscles, but his gorgeous eyes glowed. 'Maybe.'

'I can imagine it. You'll be stern and thoughtful and *très très vraiment* strict.'

He grinned at her mimicry. '*Me— Zut*, I am thinking of that ultrasound. It will be—amazing.'

'I know,' she breathed. 'To hear the little heartbeat.'

He grabbed her hand. 'Come. I'm not ready to be with other people. Let's go where we can talk.'

The Ritz wasn't to hand, but luckily there was a patisserie on the next corner, Le Brioche d'Or. As they approached the crowded café Shari heard some jazz being played within. As if her heart wasn't high enough.

All the aromas made her mouth water. Though ravenous after her scant breakfast, she was mindful of the upcoming lunch. It would be a serious social solecism not to eat at Laraine's on this occasion. So she confined herself to selecting only tea and a miniature *tarte aux pommes* from the pastry counter. Luc ordered coffee.

Sliding into a booth in the upper room at a window overlooking the street, Shari spread out the information pamphlets and selected one, only raising her head when the food was delivered.

The tea was weak and watery, but these days that was how she liked it. She cut the pastry into two pieces and shoved one across to Luc. While perusing a screed about suggested dietary modifications for pregnancy, she bit into her scrumptious flaky pastry. Luckily there was nothing on the forbidden list about butter, apple a squidgin on the tart side, or rich heavenly custard.

The entire *tarte* was the sheerest bliss. She felt so sorry for all the people in the world who weren't in Paris with Luc. She eyed his untouched piece.

'Are you sure you want that?'

Without looking up the gorgeous man passed it back to her.

'Thank you. This one's in French only,' she murmured, applying her paper napkin to the corner of her mouth. 'Though I can manage most of it. You know, if I'm going to have this baby here I'll have to enrol in some French lessons.'

Luc glanced up from the booklet he'd been perusing. 'If? What is this *if*?'

'Oh.' Jolted, she met his sharp gaze. 'Well… It's just a fig-ure of speech. I've booked into the clinic now so—I guess I'm—having the baby here.' She grinned reassuringly. 'If I can fix my visa.'

He glanced away from her. When he looked back again his eyes were veiled. 'And you're content—with that?'

'You mean—am I content with *tu*?' She smiled at his search-ing gaze. 'I am. I'm quite content.'

He returned to his reading. Glancing at him a couple of times, she noticed his brows edging closer and closer together. Was it something she'd said?

The next time he spoke, he sounded his usual calm self. 'Why were you thinking about this amnio needle test? Are you concerned there might be something wrong?'

'Oh, no.' She sighed, then pressed her lips together. 'I don't even want to think about anything like that.' She hesitated, then blurted something that had been nagging at the edge of her mind. 'The thing is, apart from checking for abnormali-ties, the test can also determine the baby's DNA.'

'So?'

She gazed at him. 'Maybe we should have it. Just to—settle any tiny little doubts you might have.'

His eyes glinted. 'I don't have any doubts.'

She could feel her pulse beating a little too fast, but she dis-ciplined her voice to stay serene and reasonable.

'Still, the question has been raised between us, and I—I—well, just for my own peace of mind—need to know that if I'm staying here with you, if we are together in this, you have no reason to doubt me.'

With a rueful expression, he reached across the table and grabbed her hand. '*Chérie*, I don't doubt you. I don't doubt you at all.'

She covered their clasped hands with her free one. 'That's lovely of you to say, Luc, but I'm thinking ahead to when this baby is born. What if he or she doesn't immediately resemble you? Or what if I can see the resemblance, but you can't? Don't you see? I'm quite an affectionate person. By that time I'll have spent nearly a year of my life with you, and I could probably end up being really quite—attached to you by then. If that happened and you doubted me, I wouldn't be able to bear it. The ending would be bad. *Big* time.'

He concealed his lowered gaze behind his dark lashes, frowning deeply. The moment stretched and stretched until her nerves nearly snapped.

Finally he said, 'If you think it will bring you peace of mind...' He threw out his hands. '*D'accord.*'

D'accord? Just like that?

Like a sandbagged zombie, she poured more milk into her tea and made it even weaker. If coffee wasn't recommended, tea probably shouldn't be either. And if a man agreed to having a DNA test to verify his paternity without a fuss, surely that was for the best.

N'est-ce pas?

Even if the test had the barest, most infinitesimal possibility of endangering the child's very existence?

CHAPTER THIRTEEN

'YOU'RE very quiet.' They were crossing the Seine en route to *chez Laraine*. 'Was it all too much? Are you feeling well?'

'Sure. I'm feeling great. Just—thinking, is all.'

Thinking about what an idiot she was. Why had she done it? She'd set up a trap and walked straight into herself. She didn't *want* that ghastly test unless the doctor specifically recommended it.

It only served her right for angling for reassurance. And how useless that had been. If a man wasn't in love, he wasn't, and nothing would ever make it happen.

At least he wasn't lying to her. She supposed she should respect his implacable resistance to swearing undying love he didn't mean.

With a sick feeling she realised that if she didn't take the test, Luc would assume she was scared of the outcome.

'This may not be the best time for you to go to lunch when you have had such a strenuous morning,' he said apologetically, 'but on any normal day I'll be at work. I'm not sure you're ready to visit Maman on your own. What do you think?'

Shari glanced quickly at him. *Her*? Visit Maman on her own? Had he been eating the wrong mushrooms?

'You may be right,' was all she said. But her mental cogs were whirring like crazy. Was this to be her lot from now on? Regular visits into the jaws of hell? Not that they were unkind to her there. It was just that her status with them was so uncertain. She wasn't quite a cousin, nor yet a *fiancée*. Perhaps she was a girlfriend, although surely Frenchmen loved their girlfriends.

'What am I?' she said.

He looked sharply at her. '*Comment*?'

'How do I explain myself to your family? I mean…it's hard to know where I stand there. Am I a friend of the family?'

'Of course you are a friend. You are—*my*…' Seemed he too had trouble finding the word. 'It will be easier for you when you learn more French,' he said suavely. 'Everything will be easier.'

After twice making an exhibition of herself before his entire family, she seriously doubted that. It would take some magnificent achievement, like saving France from invasion, or reconstituting Napoleon, to correct the impression she'd made.

'Exactly how much does your mother know?' she said lightly as he backed the Merc into an impossibly tight space in the vicinity of the building.

'She knows nothing. Or…' He lifted his hands from the wheel. 'She is Maman. She could know everything.' He flashed her a grin.

Great.

'Think of it this way,' he said smoothly, urging her up his mother's garden path. 'Now you are staying in Paris you will need to know some people. When I am at my office all day, you might need a friend to talk to. Here are some people who are willing to know you.'

Shari broke into a laugh. Her heart warmed with love for the sweet man. At least he was thoughtful about her loneliness. And his excitement about the baby was a fantastic relief.

Fortunately, this visit was less nerve-wracking than the first. She'd done everything humanly possibly here to dispel the notion she was Rémy's woman on her first visit, and today it paid off. No urns were on display, and the assembly around the lunch table treated her with kid gloves.

She guessed that those who hadn't been present the first

time she visited had been apprised of her dive into the twi-
light zone.

Strolling in with Luc, she tried to look reassuringly normal
and joyous. Certainly, after the visit to the doctor, some joy
must have still been hanging about her because it kept trilling
through her spirit. Nothing too terrible could touch her with
Luc's enthusiasm for their shared secret wrapped around her
heart like a shield.

'*Alors*, Shari, how are you today?' people said after the exchange of kissing. 'Are you well, *ma chérie*? Are you eating
your food?'

Laraine herself, dressed in a lovely linen suit, was very at-
tentive to Shari's comfort. Shari wondered if it was an accident the decanter of mineral water had been positioned near
her place setting. How was a woman able to be so charming,
so intelligent, so pleasant and discreet all at the same time, and
still be so formidable?

At least Shari felt more confident about her clothes. She was
wearing her floral dress, heels, and had wound her hair into a
chignon to show off some aquamarine earrings Luc had surprised her with in honour of their first consultation.

She'd drawn a caterpillar on her collarbone, but felt pretty
sure it would only be visible if she leaned forward, or had to
twist about.

Laraine's cast of characters had expanded. There was a
new couple, Raoul and Lucette. Lucette had a baby in a high
chair she was feeding while attempting to eat her own food.
Every so often Raoul interrupted his conversation to amuse
the baby or assist in the production of shovelling food into his
little rosebud mouth. Whenever Raoul looked on them a softness touched his eyes.

He loves him, Shari thought, trying not to stare. Really loves
him. And he loves her.

Tante Marise was late to arrive, and after she'd kissed and
been kissed by everyone she exclaimed to Luc, '*Again,* Luc,

and so soon. We are honoured, *hein*?' Then she turned to Shari, her blue eyes so genuinely kind Shari felt warmed. 'I am so happy you are here, Shari. When do you return to Australia?'

Shari felt Luc's quick glance. 'Not yet. Not for a while.'

'*Oh, là*, but where are you staying? Not in an 'otel?'

'Shari is staying with me,' Luc said, taking up a ladle and turning to Shari. '*Tagine, chérie*?'

All eyes sparkled and flitted between Luc and Shari. After a polite nodded 'Ah' from Tante Marise, conversations about half a dozen random subjects broke out while the family digested the information with their *tagine à l'orange*.

Chickpeas and lentils in a mildly aromatic sauce.

Delicious.

Shari felt a pleased glow. She could have kissed the man right there. A public acknowledgement of their relationship, however discreet, was a breakthrough.

Laraine seemed to take the news in her stride. She merely nodded, as if her son was confirming something she'd suspected all along. Her glance at Shari continued warm, curious, a little amused, and Shari felt it often.

She supposed mothers worried about who was birthing their sons' babies. By some feat of witchcraft, Laraine had already guessed she was in the family way. How soon would be tactful to fill the matriarch in officially? Not understanding how things worked between mother and son made the territory chancy.

Until Luc was ready to declare his paternity to the world, Shari couldn't feel any real security. And how likely was he to announce it loud and clear unless he knew for certain he was the father?

By the time they were through the salad course, Rochefort and were embarking on the *mousse aux framboises*, Rémy's name hadn't been mentioned once. The family were making an effort.

Maybe a day would come when she would feel relaxed with them all and stop worrying about every little thing. But after she and Luc had said their farewells, kissed and been kissed, the burning question had crystallised in her mind.

When would she return home? Would she *ever*?

'It wasn't quite so scary this time,' she said to Luc afterwards.

'It was good you remained conscious,' he agreed, smiling.

'And the earrings helped.'

'Tu étais belle. Soon they will love you.'

Her heart panged. Would they?

Would he?

She twisted her hands in her lap. 'It feels strange not to know for certain where I'll be in a year's time. Or if I'll be seeing Neil at Christmas.'

He looked sharply at her. 'You'll be *here* at Christmas. With me. On the very brink of giving birth, if not in the hospital.'

'*If* we can arrange the visa.'

'Don't worry about that, *chérie.* You worry far too much. I'm meeting with someone tomorrow, and we will discuss it.'

'Someone in the government?'

His eyes veiled and he waggled his hand. 'A friend.' After a long silence he observed casually, 'You and Neil must be— very close.'

'Well, naturally. He practically brought me up, you know.'

He was silent so long, she turned to examine him. He was far away, a curious twist to his mouth.

'Now who's looking worried,' she teased. 'Lighten up. I'm the one giving birth.'

Eager to fit in, she enrolled in intensive French lessons. Five mornings a week she caught the métro to Saint-Placide where she brushed up on her vocabulary and grammar. It didn't seem to help when she was on the train eavesdropping on people's conversations, but at least she was learning things about French manners and customs that hadn't been included at high school.

Luc was pleased. And she began to notice that, more and

more, he reverted to his own language when they were conversing.

Gradually, words and expressions must have been seeping into her understanding, because often she caught his meaning. Not that she understood *him* any the better, except in the matter of passion, where understanding flowed between them like a tumultuous river.

The first ultrasound scan was an unforgettable experience. The indistinct and everchanging images of a tiny burgeoning person, the brave little rhythm of another heart beating within her had a deeply emotional effect on them both. During the event Luc seemed to lose all power of speech. Shari naturally cried, but glancing at Luc at one point she caught an awed shimmer in his eyes too, though he quickly concealed them from her.

The news was good. The baby was developing well, and growing at the normal rate. The doctor offered to tell them the gender, but seeing a doubt in Luc's shining eyes, Shari said softly, 'I think we'd like to be surprised.'

Before they left, the doctor paused. 'Everything is looking very strong. Your next ultrasound will be in July.' She produced a schedule with all Shari's future consultations listed. The amniocentesis test hadn't been included, to Shari's relief.

Maybe she could just quietly forget about it. Pretend the subject had never come up. But her relief was shortlived when the doctor added, 'I see no need for the amnio test you inquired about. Your risk level is very low. Unless you have some concerns you wish to settle?'

Shari tensed. 'No, no. I just…' She glanced at Luc, who'd frowned. She could feel a blush creep up her neck and into her hair. Admitting to the doctor that the father of her child had ever had the slightest question about his paternity, rightly or wrongly, was harder than she'd even imagined. 'Can we make the decision later?'

Luc scoured Shari's troubled face. He said gently, 'We don't need to have the test, you know.'

The doctor looked from one to the other, her intelligent glance veiled.

'We'll discuss it again,' Shari told her, cheeks blazing. 'I'll let you know.'

'*Bien sûr*,' the doctor said easily. 'I will write it in and we can always eliminate it if we decide to.'

They would decide to, Luc thought, pierced by Shari's blush. Somehow he would persuade her out of it. He thought guiltily back to the day he'd snapped at her in the café. He'd planted that seed of insecurity in her himself with his own careless tongue. Added to the Rémy effect…

Was it any wonder she believed he didn't trust her?

It was a delicate balancing act, keeping a woman happy and secure without making her feel as pinned as a butterfly. How did guys achieve it? With a cold anxious burr it occurred to him that if he wasn't careful she'd be on the next plane to Australia.

And then what?

A flash of his life before she came into it chilled his soul like a sudden arctic breeze. He wouldn't let her go. Not without a fight.

'I wish I didn't have to return to work,' he said thickly out in the street, pausing to shower her face in kisses. 'I want to be with you. I could have you right here against this lamppost.'

'Flattering, but would it be wise, *monsieur*? I'd rather not be arrested.'

He laughed, but, surrendering to her protest, escorted her to the car with his arm around her waist, brimming with positive energy that communicated itself to Shari.

'Now we know we are safe we can begin to tell our friends, *n'est-ce pas*?'

Shari nodded excitedly. 'Good. I can't wait to tell Neil. He and Em'll be over the *moon*. But…' She shot him a glance. 'I think it might be best for your mother to hear it from us first.'

His dark eyes shimmered with some mysterious knowledge. 'Ah, *oui*. Maman will like you to tell her. And we must start some serious planning. We need to research the schools. And you've never said... Do we want a nanny? And I'm wondering if we need to hire a dietician to prepare your meals from now on. What do you think?'

She stared incredulously at him.

'No?' He burst into an amused laugh. 'But I *am* thinking of hiring a car with a driver for you. You shouldn't be travelling on the métro. It's too much of a risk. Anything could happen.'

'Now just hold on there. I *like* catching the...'

Luc stiffened momentarily and the words died on Shari's lips.

A taxi had drawn in behind their car and a woman got out to help another alight. When the second one straightened up Shari saw she was heavily pregnant, moving with the changed gait brought about by the redistribution of body weight. She was in jeans and heels, her enormous bump lovingly outlined by a tightly fitted shirred top. Her hair had been cut in a short, sleek, very chic bob, and she wore minimal jewellery, apart from some bangles and hoops in her ears.

Noticing Luc, she teetered backwards on her heels for an instant, and Luc lunged forward to steady her. He barely had time to touch her elbow before her companion stepped in and took a firm steadying grip of her other arm.

With a sharp pang Shari recognised that face. Who else at her advanced stage of pregnancy could manage to be so elegant? And she was, Shari acknowledged. Truly elegant. With a glowing, luminous beauty.

Luc smiled, though there was a hard glint in his narrowed eyes.

'Ah. Manon. What a magnificent surprise,' he said in French.

The beauty inclined her head. 'Luc.'

'Imagine meeting you here, of all places.' How could such

suave and graceful words be so punishing? 'And looking so—robust. Not bored with America, I trust?'

Manon glanced quickly at her friend, then pushed back her sunglasses. Her gorgeous amber eyes were defiant. 'I could never be bored with America. But where else does one go at this beautiful time of life?'

Her glance flicked sideways to Shari for a bare instant, then back to him.

There was a screechingly silent abyss when no one said anything, then the other woman tugged at Manon and hustled her into the clinic.

On the trip home, the atmosphere in the Merc had a certain explosive fragility. It crept in upon Shari that her situation was really very precarious. It was terrifying to think, but there was a horrible possibility about the man she loved she needed to take into account.

If he was still fixated on Manon, how long would he be likely to stay with *her*? Until the birth? Until the babe was a week old? Three months? And if he left her, would he be content to leave his baby behind?

A familiar claw caught her entrails in a death grip. She knew nothing of French law in the matter of child custody. But how likely was it that a mother—who wasn't even a citizen—would take precedence over the father who *was*?

In one swoop the excitement of the fantastic visit to the clinic was wiped.

'She's very beautiful,' she said, fluttering her lashes to draw his attention to the fact that hers were at least as long as Manon's. 'More beautiful than her pictures.' He made no answer, but she persevered. 'Did you know she was pregnant?'

His dark eyes were cool and veiled. 'I may have heard.'

'It's—quite a coincidence.'

'How is it a coincidence?'

'Well…you and she were together. Now *she's* pregnant, and here you and I are…'

'Life goes on. And...' He turned his head, and said softly, '*You* are beautiful.'

Really? If he hadn't been so angry with Manon, she might have let herself believe him. 'Was that her sister with her—some relative?'

'I can't say. I barely looked to see.' He glanced at her, his dark eyes softening. '*Chérie*, don't allow this accident of timing to bother you.'

She smiled. 'It's not. Why would it? I wish you had introduced me, though.'

'Ah. I'm sorry.'

'You could have said, "Allow me to present my pregnant friend, Shari."'

He flushed. 'Yes, I should have, but it was a shock, you know, coming upon her so—unexpectedly.'

'Mmm. I sensed that.' She compressed her lips.

'This is the first time I've seen her in seventeen, eighteen months. The last time I saw her we were...she and I were engaged in mortal combat.'

She could just imagine it. The drama and the passion. Especially the passion. 'Who was the victor?'

'Oh, Manon, *bien sûr*. A man has no chance against a woman with claws extended.'

Her heart pained. How he must have loved the beautiful woman, to feel so bitter. She wished she'd never asked.

'You must miss her,' she observed coldly.

'*Shari*.' His gentle chiding tone made her feel ashamed. Advertising her neediness was hardly the way to inspire a man to love her. She felt her throat thicken, but held back the tears for all she was worth.

The rest of the journey seethed with an unbearable silence. When they drew up in the street before their apartment building, he turned to her, his intelligent eyes alert and at the same time grave.

He hesitated, then took her hand and said firmly, 'I don't

miss her, *mon amour*. I'm with you now. I've moved on. We all have.'

'Sure. Sure we have.'

'Hold the irony, please, Mlle Lacey.' His dark eyes scrutinised her face with tender concern. 'We—Manon and I were over long before our affair ended.'

She lifted her eyebrows. '*Affair*? Oh, that's cool. After seven *years*...'

He shrugged. 'That was what she wanted our relationship to be. No promises, no certainties. More than anything in the world she didn't want to *belong* to anyone.' His mouth made a sardonic curl. 'So she *said*. That was what caused the final crash. She wanted our relationship to stay the same. But...' He opened his palms and said simply, '*I* changed. I wanted—more. I understand now she saw that as a betrayal. At the time I was—angry. Disillusioned. You might say a little bitter. I said some things that were unkind, and she—stormed off to the airport in a fury, never to return.'

'Oh.' So it wasn't just the Jackson Kerr affair that had broken their relationship. Shari hardly dared ask, but the question was burning on her tongue. 'What was it *you* wanted?'

He flicked down his lashes and made a rueful grimace. 'Not a Russian wolfhound. No. I...er...suffered a brainstorm on my way home one evening and thought I wanted to have a child. Imagine that.' He shot her a veiled glance.

Her heart started thumping with a dawning realisation, but she struggled on to extract more of this astounding confession. 'You and Manon? You *wanted* a—a—baby?'

He inclined his head.

'Oh. Right. Well. *Well. So...* Did you—propose to her?'

He shrugged. 'The roses, the ring, the carpet of rose petals, the private room in the restaurant, kneeling like a fool—the whole bloody farce.'

'Oh-h-h.' She winced in sympathy. 'And she said no?'

He gave a sardonic laugh. 'Manon was a little like you in

some of her ideas. She accused me of being a selfish chauvin-
ist determined to cruelly subjugate her to domestic slavery and
prevent her from realising her full potential by weighing her
down with children.' From the harsh intake of breath through
his nostrils, some lingering outrage was apparent. 'That was
what she said to the media, among other things.'

She could imagine how bitterly such a rejection had hurt.
Then to see Manon allowing herself to be subjugated by the
next man in so precisely the manner she'd sneered at…

Shari's heart positively ached for him. No wonder he'd been
so cold to the beauty when they'd met. 'That really wasn't fair,'
she said earnestly. 'You may not be perfect, but you aren't
cruel.'

He laughed and kissed her lips. 'Thank you, *chérie*. I am
trying very hard not to be. And the fates must have forgiven
me, because now I have an adorable…'

'Friend.'

His dark eyes gleamed. '*And* a child to look forward to. I
am the happiest father-to-be in Paris. Do you believe that?'

Meeting his glowing gaze, she did. If there was one thing
she was certain about, it was that. He was definitely in love
with the baby.

'And I'm not really like her at all, by the way,' she said, getting out of the car.

But the concierge called to him at that moment, and Shari
doubted he even heard.

Darkness was approaching when Luc strolled into a bar in a
sidestreet tucked around the corner from the Ministry for the
Interior. His elderly friend was already ensconced at a table,
perusing *Le Figaro*.

'Henri.'

'Ah, Luc.' He folded the news sheet and rose to brush cheeks.
'Good to see you, my young friend. What are we drinking?'

Henri already had a cognac before him, so Luc signalled the

bartender for the same. Once the courtesies had been observed, enquiries made about health, family and the stock market, the real reason for their meeting was subtly addressed.

'I'm afraid the news is not good for your friend with the *fiancée*.'

Luc's heart lurched. 'No?'

'There are some laws made of steel. They cannot be bent in the slightest. I'm sorry, my friend, but what can one do? This is the new world. The law is implacable on immigration matters. However...' Henri contemplated his cognac. 'Might I suggest a possible solution?'

Luc listened, and his spirits sank. Henri was assuming that this situation was straightforward, the woman like any other.

He endeavoured to explain. 'She is not—I *believe* from what my friend says—she is not the sort of woman who wishes to be pinned down. Forever is not a phrase in her vocabulary. My friend is concerned that if he sets a foot wrong she'll be fleeing to the airport in a snap.'

Henri arched his brows and laughed with frank amusement. 'Ah, Luc. Tell your friend he is an idiot. He just needs to find the right inducement.' He made a suggestive, masculine gesture. 'In the end they all want to be pinned down.'

Luc grimaced ruefully. 'Not all.' He rose, thanking Henri before leaving and walking slowly back to the métro, a heavy weight constricting his heart. 'No. Not all.'

Shari spent some of her afternoon engaged in research. It was a risk, it could have been self-defeating, but knowledge was power.

Unsurprisingly, there was little of recent date to find out about Manon. The grand passion seemed to have dropped altogether from public sight. As Shari had noticed as far back as Sydney, it seemed that once the scandal had been milked for every last drop the media circus had moved on. The tabloid sites were no longer swamped with sightings of Jackson Kerr and his new woman.

Just a view here or there of Manon spotted in Beverly Hills, always shying away from the camera. Manon sunning herself on Jackson's private beach with a friend.

Was it possible they'd split up? Was this why Manon was back in France to have her baby? Shari was ready to bet LA was dotted with fabulous clinics for celebrities. Surely the American ones would compete with the best in the world.

She studied some of the old images from the time Manon had worked for the glossy. How could Manon have even *dreamed* of exchanging Luc for a butterfly like Jackson Kerr?

Scrolling back to the Malibu image, she enlarged it so she could get a clearer view of the friend. She could have been the same woman who'd been with Manon at the clinic.

Jackson might have been off on location somewhere. Shari hoped he wasn't seducing another leading lady. He already had a few notches on his belt in that direction, if the celeb spotters were to be believed.

That would certainly explain why Manon had come back. Maybe she needed to call on friends and family for support.

When Luc arrived home Shari noticed a change in his mood. He tried to conceal it, but she sensed there was something on his mind. As if that over-the-moon excited guy in the street outside the clinic had plummeted to earth and it had gone hard with him.

She examined him carefully. 'Is everything fine? At work? Your family?'

Anxiously she contemplated the meal she'd cooked. Her salad—she was leaving the vinaigrette dressing to him—the lamb cutlets with the Shari Lacey version of ratatouille instead of a sauce. It was Luc's turn to make the dessert.

His handsome face lightened. 'Everything is good. No need to worry.' He smiled, but she couldn't help wondering. And worrying.

He partook of the meal she'd partly prepared with apparent appreciation, but, as she'd noted before, he was a courteous guy. She made the resolution to take some lessons in French cuisine just as soon as she had the chance. Definitely.

Over the next week or so he often seemed deep in meditation. Once or twice she caught him looking at her with an expression she couldn't interpret.

Well, she *was* starting to show. Her waist had thickened a little, and there were definite signs of a bump. To compensate she started making sure she looked beautilicious when he arrived home. Pretty clothes, underwear. She even had her hair cut and foiled and bought a straightener. At one point she succumbed to ironing a tee shirt.

In the bedroom she felt driven to experiment in ways that surprised even her normally inventive self. Was it hormones, rivalry or sheer insanity? Every time he looked gloomy, she felt challenged to distract him in some new and sensuous way.

She was at risk of turning herself into a femme fatale.

Luc came home early one afternoon when she was working on her book. The dining room's light with its romantic view of the rooftops and chimney pots of Paris had made it the obvious choice for her workplace. To spare the furniture, she'd spread a sheet over the table for her paints and paraphernalia, and pinned up some paper to protect the silken walls from splashes.

'*Ça va.*' He kissed her, tasting of coffee, the city, man and desire.

'You're early.'

'*Oui.*' He noticed her painting and bent to examine it, exclaiming, 'Aha. The carousel in the Luxembourg. You know, my papa used to take me there when I was a little kid.'

'Oh, did he? It's so beautiful there. It must be the best gig in the world for a juggler.'

'But I don't see your owl,' he said, searching the picture.

'Ah. No. I've abandoned him until I'm in Australia again.'

He frowned, as he often did when she mentioned Australia. She guessed the reminder of Rémy's business shenanigans there still stung like crazy.

'See?' Shyly, she showed him her initial sketch, and some beautiful old posters she'd unearthed from the famous Cirque d'hiver. 'I'm still working on the face. It's not so easy to do the juggler.'

He compared them with her painting, exclaiming about the little telltale signs she'd used to make the setting obvious to Parisian children. 'It's so good. It's…exceptional. *Magnifique.* You are a great talent.' Glancing about at her protective measures, he indicated the room with a sweep of his hand.

'Maybe you'd like to change all this. Find a new look for the apartment. Make this a proper studio.'

'But that would be so much trouble, wouldn't it, when we don't even know how long-term my stay here will be? I'd hate to cause you all that expense for something that might well turn out to be temporary.'

'*Shari*…'

She looked enquiringly at him. He looked almost pained, then his jaw hardened. He threw out his hands. '*Chérie*— There is something— I have something I must discuss with you.'

Clunk. For some reason her heart hit a pothole. She picked up a cloth and wiped her hands.

He took her shoulders and looked gravely at her. 'I have had news. Your visa can't be changed from within France. I'm sorry, *chérie*, but the laws here are very strict. If you wish to apply to be a resident, you must do it from Australia.'

'Oh.' It was a shock. 'You mean—go home? *Already*?' Disappointment, and a zillion obstacles flashed through her mind. Being with him. Their life. Her hopes and dreams. Her French lessons, her clinic appointments. Leaving him. Leaving *him*.

He lifted his hands. 'The immigration and visa laws have tightened here as everywhere. This is why…' his dark lashes screened his eyes '—I am suggesting—to spare you the trip— we should get married.'

Her brain spun for a giddy minute or so. When it slowed down she noticed a certain rigidity in him. A waiting stillness. Then the full implications of the words hit.

Pain sliced her heart like a knife. 'Oh. Oh. *Married*. Heavens, has it come to that?'

His eyes glinted. 'It may look like an extreme solution, but in your condition… Surely a long flight wouldn't be advisable?'

'Oh, that's just…' She smiled bitterly and shook her head. 'Pregnant women can fly right up until the thirty-sixth week.'

'Are you sure? How do you know?' His voice sharpened. 'Have you been checking?'

'Emilie. She wanted to come for the… Anyway… Anyway…' She laid her palm on her forehead. She felt flummoxed and prickly, as if all her fur had been horribly ruffled and she might just burst into tears. 'If I go home, who knows how long I'll have to wait for a residential visa? I'll just have the baby there, I guess.'

'*No*. No, Shari…' He made a sharp movement but she turned away from him. 'Don't think of leaving, *chérie*. No need to give up. The marriage ceremony is nothing. Just a formality. A banal, bureaucratic formality.'

'Look, I just need to think for a while. Excuse me while I go for a walk.'

She grabbed her bag and almost flew out of the apartment. Down on the ground floor she rushed blindly past the concierge's office, then headed to the nearest métro. The closest station to the Luxembourg was only one stop further on from Saint-Placide where she travelled for her lessons. Several times already she'd walked from there to the gardens to help her story cook.

Naturally, like the thoroughly emotional woman she was, she cried on the train. Then she cried on the way to the gardens, which was silly because she bumped into people and some of them were quite rude.

Then she walked past the children's garden, past the carousel, all the way to the fountain where she'd first told Luc she was expecting. As a coincidence, it was late afternoon again, not many people about.

She sank into a green chair and sat with her head in her hands. These last few weeks she'd been living in a bubble, she realised, and now it had burst.

But if you loved someone, what did it matter? A marriage proposal was a marriage proposal. She probably didn't deserve roses and pretty words and kneeling on the ground. The alternative was to leave him and fly home. Leave him without his baby? How could she even contemplate such a thing?

If she did make that long journey, would she ever come back? Would he even *want* her back?

So he wasn't 'in love'. He was a decent man. Straight, honourable and good. *Gentle.* What was she quibbling about? There were women who would give their eye teeth to be where she was. He'd be good to her, she supposed, since she was the mother of his child. His first child.

She waited for the ache in her heart to ease. Eventually the peace and beauty of the place soothed her enough that she could pull herself together. Then she hauled herself up and caught another train home.

When she walked in she noticed with surprise Luc holding a whiskey in his hand. She'd never known him to drink alcohol, other than with a meal.

He scrutinised her carefully, his eyes burning strangely in his taut face. 'Did you walk far?'

'I—went for a stroll in the Luxembourg. Thought I might as well check on something while I was in the mood for roaming. Oh, and about that other thing. Okay. I'll marry you, if you insist. But let's not make a fuss about it, eh? No white dresses and all that palaver. Just regular old clothes.'

Frowning, he looked at her uncertainly. 'Are you sure?'

She half turned away. 'Well, it's just a formality, isn't it? Let's do it without a fuss.'

'*Chérie...*'

Whatever he'd been going to say, he thought better of it.

They avoided each other's eyes after that, and there was a strain during dinner.

In their bed that night, she lay with her back to him, her heart aching too much for sleep. While Luc's breathing was steady and regular, a certain tension in him made her aware he was awake.

She tried to cry silently, until she felt his touch on her thigh and a burning, treacherous tingle ignited her blood. Desire and resistance warred in her flesh, until with a groan he reached for her and pulled her into his arms, murmuring, '*Chérie,* don't be sad. Everything will be all right.'

And once again he was the most virile, passionate and demanding of lovers. He rode her, he owned her, he possessed her like a king. Then he changed tack and became the warmest, the tenderest, the most considerate.

In his powerful arms she melted, she surrendered, she showed him all the love blazing in her soul. And from the tenderness in his embrace, anyone would have thought the man truly loved her.

CHAPTER FOURTEEN

'I'M NOT so sure about wearing old clothes to our wedding, *chérie.*'

Shari scowled. Until this moment she'd been enjoying her breakfast. Until this moment croissants and toast had never tasted so good. She was doing her best to be gracious over the travesty of a wedding she was forced to settle for, but that didn't mean she should have to discuss it when she had serious things on her mind.

Things like wilfully endangering her baby just to pander to some totally unfounded suspicions. Sure, it had been her suggestion, based on an insane and quixotic impulse, but the fact that Luc was going along with it *even after* he'd thoroughly read that pamphlet, interrogated the doctor to within an inch of the poor woman's life and researched the whole question on the Internet ad infinitum spoke for itself.

He still didn't one hundred per cent trust her.

And if he didn't, how could he ever love her? She knew from her own bitter experience the end of trust meant the end of love.

In this case, love had never begun.

Despite all his affectionate words and gestures, his concern for her well-being, his apparent pride when he introduced her to people, he'd never once been tempted to say he loved her, when she, on so many occasions, had only just managed not to embarrass him with heartfelt outpourings of eternal love by severely restraining herself.

Oh, there'd been moments in the heat of passion when he'd come on pretty strong about how he adored her, she'd changed his life, et cetera, but she knew the difference, and so did a sophisticated guy like him.

He couldn't even claim it was a cultural idiosyncrasy at work. Everyone knew the French were renowned for their passionate declarations. For heaven's sake, hadn't they invented the language of love?

Even in Australia, where men feared to string more than two words together at a time in case of being thought female, they managed to say deep and soulful things to their lovers in private. Behind closed doors. With the blinds down.

This whole amniocentesis thing was another symbol of her failure to inspire love in a man. It was shaming to think some women were forced to go through the procedure for very urgent and genuine reasons, while she'd signed on for little more than as a test to prove herself.

To prove she wasn't a liar. How sad was that?

Paradoxically, she suspected Luc wasn't comfortable with the idea himself. But it had become another of those things they didn't talk about. Like love.

'It occurs to me…' he said, casually spooning double cream onto the jam he'd spread inside his croissant. How could the man stay so lean and fit? *His* abdomen was as flat as a washboard. '…That our witnesses are likely to use the occasion of our wedding as an excuse to strut their finery.'

'Well, then, it's a pity we can't choose witnesses who aren't *prone* to finery. Like perfect strangers walking along the street.'

Though his dark eyes shimmered, his face continued grave. 'Yes, that is a shame. Strangers would have been perfect. Unfortunately, the law has spoken. Perhaps we can strike a compromise. Suppose tomorrow we take a stroll through the boutiques? There must be something in Paris you could enjoy wearing to your wedding. A suit. A dress.'

'I doubt it.'

The truth was, any control she'd had over the event was fast slipping away. Already she'd been forced to give in on the witness question.

The law was stacked against her. During several visits to the *mairie*, her situation in regard to her Australian birth and the inadequacy of her visa had occasioned some terse comments from the *conseiller municipal* who was to perform the ceremony.

Could she prove her relationship with Luc was genuine and not just an attempt to marry a French citizen by devious means? Could she *prove* she had genuine links with France and deserved special consideration?

The doctor's certification that she was pregnant, and had certainly been pregnant before she left Australia, possibly coinciding with Luc's documented visit there, only went part of the way to assuage official doubts. Even the dozen or so Australian documents she'd sent home for, along with Luc's documents, were held as doubtful.

Her relationship by marriage to Luc's cousin Emilie was counted as helpful. Even more helpful would be the endorsement of other members of Luc's immediate family.

Though Luc argued fiercely with the officials about the ridiculous red tape and bureaucracy that was strangling France and its citizens, he accepted the ruling.

Shari wasn't sure how regretful he truly was when he announced they were forced to invite two members of his family to be their witnesses.

'What can I say?' he'd raged when he broke the news, striding up and down and flinging out his hands. 'We live in a paranoid society in which citizens are considered guilty before being proven innocent. I'm so sorry, my darling, but our hands are tied. This is why I'm leaving it to you to decide who we should honour with the role.'

Shari frowned. 'Two?'

'*Bien sûr*, the law requires two.'

Two of his family. It wasn't that she disliked his family. They'd been very kind on every occasion. Since their announcement of the baby, both the Sophies had invited her to go shopping with them, Raoul and Lucette had invited her and Luc to dinner, and Laraine had called by to drink tea. During the visit the gracious woman had expressed her sincere condolences about all the yellow silk.

'It doesn't suit every complexion,' she'd said sympathetically. 'I'm not sure it even suited Manon. And it can be very wearing on the nerves. Probably on relationships, I wouldn't be surprised. Make a couple a little irritable, *hein*? I know my son has always detested yellow. In your case, *ma chérie*, a warm white, pale cream, perhaps even a *très, très* watery shade of blue could be to your advantage.'

Laraine was right about one thing. Yellow was irritating.

In fact, ever since Luc had made the proposal, if anyone could call it that, things that hadn't bothered Shari before bothered her now. That was one good reason why this so-called wedding didn't deserve to be classed as a celebration.

She tried not to look at him, all crisp and fresh in his city suit, his handsome jaw cleanly shaven while she was still a classic frump in one of his old tee shirts and straggly hair. It wasn't fair that a man should always be beautiful.

He was absorbed in reading his tablet, but every so often he remembered she was alive. 'Have you thought any more about the witnesses, *chérie*?' he said absently. 'We will have to give them some warning.'

'I'm not sure who in your family would have the *time* for such a banal formality. It's hardly a social event. Merely the signing of a contract.

Behind their dark lashes his eyes glinted. 'It shouldn't be impossible to find two who are willing. I dare say everyone in my family would *like* to witness my wedding.'

She glanced at him, but his face was entirely innocent as he perused *Le Figaro*, making occasional stabbing gestures with his forefinger at articles that infuriated him.

'Well…' She studied her toast, which could have been improved by a very thin smear of Vegemite, if only the French knew it. 'I suppose it would be nice to ask your mother.'

There was a moment of silence. Then, 'You think?'

She said gloomily, 'Though if we ask her, we can't possibly *not* ask Tante Marise.'

He nodded. 'Although Oncle Georges would be overjoyed to be included. Still, it's difficult with only the two. But what can one do? Papa is in Venice, but even he might feel he has a claim…'

She could see the crack widening in the dam wall. ' I *suppose*…one *could* invite some of them as guests.'

He glanced up, his face illuminated with a sudden devastating smile that wrung her heart. 'Only if you would feel comfortable with that, of course.'

She shrugged, gracious in defeat. At least he could be happy. 'Oh, sure, sure. Invite them all. And the children. *And* their dogs. But you know what that means, don't you?'

He was smiling at his iPad. 'What?'

'Printed invitations. Flowers. Photos. Receptions. All that stuff. Stuff I know nothing about arranging.'

'You can leave all that to me. What about Neil and Emilie?'

'Are you kidding? The twins are barely three months old. Em won't want to travel with them. And she's breastfeeding so she can't leave them behind, even if she wanted to. No, I'm doomed to go it alone.'

'Tsk, tsk. So depressing. At least on Saturday we can see about your dress. That will be something beautiful to think of, *n'est-ce pas*?'

She heaved a bored sigh. 'Whatever. Choose what you like. Just so long as it's yellow.'

She could tell she'd made some impact with that. He looked at her long and hard.

But it gave her no real satisfaction. Did she want to disgruntle him and send him off to the office looking stern for another day of terrifying his employees? No, she wanted him to be happy. She wanted him to have everything in the world he wanted. Even if it wasn't her, all that much.

Of course, once she had proved her case about his paternity, he might see her in a different light. If she didn't throw herself off the Pont Neuf first.

After he'd kissed her goodbye, then strode off to catch his train, she drifted around for a while, half-heartedly tidying things like a nineteen fifties housewife and feeling miserable about the whole damned thing.

It was lowering to know that a man would never have dreamed of marrying you if you hadn't been pregnant. And just to underline that fact couldn't even be bothered to dress up his proposal with a few flowery words.

Lately, she'd even given up the effort to dress herself up. Most days she mooched around in shorts, shirts and sandals, her hair in a daggy ponytail. Occasionally she'd drag on a skirt for the shops, but that was her biggest concession.

She felt Luc's gaze on her often, anxious, troubled, but she didn't feel like explaining. If he couldn't work out that a woman liked to feel at least *equal* to his ex in his regard, what was the point?

There was an evening when Luc was taking her to a reception at the Turkish embassy. When she emerged from her boudoir in a shortish skirt and a vest top, Luc stood stock still, gorgeous in his evening suit, surveying her quite sternly. Then he steered her back into her dressing room, stripped off those clothes and pulled out her good black dress.

'Put this on,' he commanded, then added smoothly, 'They will be going to some trouble for us. We have to consider their feelings too, *mon amour*.' Though gentle, there was unmistakable steel in his demeanour.

She knew she was sulking like an angry, disappointed child,

but that was because she was an angry, disappointed woman, with a child inside. While she capitulated in the matter of the dress, in a bold act of defiance she painted a fly on her cheek.

Luc simply smiled and said, 'Enchanting.' And to further destabilise her, he introduced her to all the dignitaries at the reception as his future bride with apparent glowing pride.

The rift stretched between them as wide and cold as a frozen sea.

Her blue mood persisted until the day of the amnio test. On the morning of the test she was jumpier than a cricket. Since her appointment at the clinic wasn't until early afternoon, she killed time by going to the market.

In an effort to crush down the jagged rocks in her chest, she visited her favourite art-supply shop first, and purchased some gentian blue and vermilion. Then she wended her way through the market, collecting sundry fruits and vegetables for the household supply. Shopping was easier now she could ask for things in French.

She was just gazing wistfully into the window of a patisserie she knew she should avoid when a voice she vaguely recognised accosted her.

'Shari, is it?'

She turned. Like an apparition from her worst nightmares, Manon was standing there, smiling a little uncertainly, an elegant tote bag hanging off her wrist.

'Oh. *Bonjour.* How are you? I mean you…you look very well. Beautiful, as always.'

Manon laughed. '*Beautiful.* I feel like a whale. My back aches, my ankles are swelling, and I'm hot. I've only just arrived and already I need to sit down. Shall we go inside?'

Shari only just managed not to drop her jaw. But why not? Why refuse the elegant woman?

'How close are you to your time?' she enquired over the tiny sliver of gateau that she'd allowed herself. No added cream. Even on a horrible day some lines had to be drawn.

'Three days past. My waters could break at any second. Does that give you an uncomfortable feeling?' She grinned and Shari allowed herself to relax and laugh. 'I'm not supposed to go out but I needed to escape. My partner would be cross with me if she could see me now.'

Shari pricked up her ears. Well, well, well. Here was an intriguing turn-up. She wondered if she should tell Luc that he and Jackson Kerr had been supplanted by a woman.

'Was that her at the clinic that day?'

Manon nodded. '*Oui*, that was Jenny. And are you and Luc still living around the corner?'

'Yep.'

'I enjoyed living there. Such a wonderful part of the city.' She smiled across her strawberry mousse.

Shari lowered her gaze. 'Mmm. I love the views.' And the man. So much. Too much.

'*Vraiment*. So pretty. I still think of my peaches and lemons sometimes. It was Luc's maman who whispered Luc's favourite colours to me.'

Shari lifted her brows. 'Really?'

'*Oui*. I could never really grow used to it. And after all my effort I was never even sure he noticed. *Men*. What can we do about them?' She gave a Gallic shrug, then winked. 'I have found my own way.'

Shari looked searchingly at her. 'And—you're happy?'

'Never happier.' The glowing radiance of her smile was undeniable. 'Life is too short not to be as happy as you can be.'

Shari agreed with that philosophy with all her heart. Though why did other people's happiness always make the heart twinge? 'Do you mind if I ask something?'

'*Mais non*. Ask away.'

'Did you have the—amniocentesis test?'

Manon nodded. 'I needed to. We had some concerns at one stage about spina bifida, because it is in my family genetics.

But…it seems there was no need to worry, after all. It's good to know our baby escaped that terrible thing.'

'How bad was it? Taking the test?'

She waggled her hand. '*Comme ci, comme ça.* A little scary. Everything is scary when you've never done it before. But in the end—not bad. It gave us peace of mind.'

'Of course.' If only *she* had peace of mind. She was beginning to doubt that a test would deliver it, when all was said and done. Feeling Manon's curious gaze, she hastened to change the subject.

'Is Jackson Kerr as gorgeous as he looks on the silver screen?'

Manon laughed. '*No.* He looks hot, but that's where it stops. He's selfish, his breath smells like a drain, and he thinks about nothing except his beauty, his personal trainer, and football. Always football. And his *mother.*' She shuddered. 'Luc is a much sweeter, smarter guy.' She added softly, 'But not the one for me.'

Heartsore on that subject, Shari lowered her lashes.

Manon scraped the bottom of her glass with the spoon. 'Someone has told me you are an author of children's books?'

'Oh, well…' Shari certainly didn't want to boast, but, under duress, she admitted it.

It was an illuminating conversation. Perhaps because they didn't need to be rivals, Manon was warm and genuinely friendly. After they'd canvassed pregnancies, partners and partners' mothers thoroughly, Shari saw her into a taxi and turned for home.

Somehow during that forty or so minutes she'd reached a decision. Cruel though it was to face the truth, she saw with clarity that clinging to a man in the hope some day her love would be returned in full measure was a fool's game. Experience had shown her that pain would only escalate with time. And life was short. Take Rémy, for instance. Here one day, gone the next.

Luc, beautiful man that he was, had done his best to do the honourable thing. He deserved a chance to find a woman he could prize as he'd prized Manon.

Somehow she'd allowed her Rémy period to sabotage her confidence and her belief in herself. The damned fool test was a case in point. How an intelligent person could have tied herself up in knots over it was nothing short of amazing.

On the walk home, she phoned the clinic and cancelled her appointment. Back in the apartment, she booked her flight to Australia, then started to gather her things. She was in the kitchen unpinning her sketches from the fridge when she heard Luc's key turn in the door, far earlier than expected.

'Shari? Are you here?'

'In the kitchen.' She braced herself, her heart thumping like a big bass drum.

When he walked in, his dark eyes were serious and unexpectedly stern. Her heart skipped a beat. What was it?

'Ça va,' he said, kissing her. He continued to hold her arms firmly, his eyes intent on her face. 'Shari, I can't let you do it.'

She started. '*What*?'

He shook his head. 'I'm sorry, my darling. I know you feel this is important for *us*, but nothing about us is as important as this little one in here.' He patted her bump tenderly.

'Oh, the test. Yes, I know, and that's exactly—'

'No, *chérie*. I need you to listen. I know you've been driving yourself crazy over this. Why are we doing it?'

She was winding up to explain her change of heart, but he went on regardless.

'It isn't necessary. I *know* you are not a liar. I've always known—what you are. Who. Who you are to me. And I won't let you leave me.'

'*Comment*?' A guilty blush heated her cheeks. Had the guy inherited his mother's terrible clairvoyance?

His face tautened. 'I—I only agreed because I wanted you so much to stay, but as far as we know it's not a medical necessity, is it? Some people need to go through this thing, but we've already decided to go ahead and have our baby, whatever the test uncovers. We said that, didn't we?'

'I know, we did. I only suggested having it in the first place because I've been feeling so insecure. Anxious.' She flushed a little. 'It was ridiculous. I couldn't be certain you trusted me. But I decided today that you'll just have to take my word for it, and if you *can't*...'

His eyes sharpened. 'But of course I take your word. And in the end,' he added hoarsely, 'who cares who our baby resembles or what selection of genes she has? Or *he* has? We'll love her, or him, because he belongs to us.'

'Oh, Luc. Oh, my darling, darling man, that's so wonderful to hear.' Tears sprang into her eyes. She put her arms around his neck and kissed him passionately, long and deep.

She could feel his hard body pressed against her, his big heart thumping with the force of his emotion. Her own was thundering fit to burst.

'I don't think you know how much I love you, Shari Lacey,' he said gruffly when they at last surfaced. 'And how I—need you.'

'Honestly?' she breathed, hardly able to believe her ears. Her heart swelled.

'*Bien sûr.*' He held her face between his hands, his brows earnestly drawn. 'You have warmed my life.'

'Oh.' Thrilling with a tremulous, painful joy she blinked madly to hold back the tears. 'Is that really true?'

He searched her face. 'How can you not know?' He spread his hands in rueful amazement. 'You won't believe it, but I used to consider myself a hard guy. Cynical, even. With you I've turned into a—a *putty*. I don't recognise myself. I've become dependent on the sound of your voice. Your—face in the morning.' His voice cracked slightly. 'At work I—I find myself thinking of you, worrying you won't be here when I come home. Even today I...' He shook his head, then looked firmly at her. 'Listen to me…' He was breathing rather hard, and his eyes grew stern and serious. 'Don't dream of walking out that door. I won't *let* you. I'll hunt you down, if necessary. I'll chase the plane you leave on. I'll pursue you to the ends of the earth.'

While she contemplated this exciting scenario, he muttered to himself, 'All along I've been so scared of losing you, I've been agreeing to crazy things like a—a madman.'

She had a fleeting vision of the time he'd raced to the Ritz at midnight to pick up some buttery scrambled eggs, but dismissed that as an example. Any man would have done the same.

She gave a gurgle of laughter through her tears. 'Oh, I wouldn't say *madman*.'

'*Oui, oui*. It's true. Every time we've disagreed over anything I've held my breath for fear you would run for the airport.'

'Oh, my poor darling.' Her heart ached with love and remorse, and a degree of guilt. 'My poor Luc. Why would you think that?'

'*Why*?' His handsome face softened. 'Shari, chérie, I've heard it in your voice. Seen it in your eyes. How you miss Neil… How you long for Australia. I understand how cold it feels in a strange country with only me to cling to.'

She gazed at the gorgeous hunk of man through her tears. 'Well, you are something worth clinging to, you know,' she said shakily. 'You don't need to worry about Neil. Of course I miss him and Em, but you…I'm in love with you. Isn't it obvious ? You're all I've ever wanted. You're the kindest, the most sexy, the hottest, the most…'

His voice thickened. 'While you are the most desirable, the most confusing, clever, adorable, darling woman…'

Joy was such a powerful aphrodisiac. This was a precious moment, a solemn, soulful moment when hearts were open and truth was on the table. The most thrilling words she would ever hear in her life were being spoken to her by the most gorgeous man in the world, yet in her delirious state of sunshine and supreme happiness she was feeling aroused.

So inappropriate. And so fantastically promising.

'I know I've been difficult,' she breathed. 'So emotional. Even now I'm feeling far too passionate. Is there any way I can make it up to you?'

'Yes,' he said fiercely. He swept her up in his arms and carried her to the bedroom.

Afterwards, when passion was for the moment in abeyance and she was lying with her head on his chest, contemplating the incredible fact that she'd misinterpreted so much about him, she said, 'I should have told you sooner how I felt. But I was afraid you were still in love with Manon.'

'No. Though I admit I felt—hurt, or something. We were over long before we split. I didn't really even understand that until the day in the café when you asked me about her. That day I brought you home and *you* nearly ran away as well.'

She squeezed his bicep. It didn't even leave a dent. 'Were you surprised when she took off with Jackson Kerr?'

He grimaced. 'Hardly. The guy's a stud. Isn't that what you women think?'

'He might well be for all I know. He *is* cute. Nice abs.' She laughed. 'Sorry. Just teasing. No, actually…' She took a deep breath. 'You may get a bit of a shock at what I'm about to tell you.'

She related the story Manon had told her in the patisserie, about falling in love and knowing it was the right thing for her.

Luc sat bolt upright as if electrified. 'What? Are you serious? She *told* you this?'

Shari nodded. 'She did. She told me things you wouldn't believe.'

'What things? Things about me?'

'No, no. Other things.' Realising she'd come close to saying too much for any macho guy to take on board at one time, she gave him a womanly glance to warn him off sacred ground. 'What we call in Australia secret women's business.'

'*Comment*?' His brows bristled with intrigue.

'Put it this way.' She hesitated, casting about for words. 'Her affair with Jackson Kerr was just a flash in the pan. Doomed to extinguish itself while she was working herself out.'

'Ah.' Luc's brows zoomed high and he looked keenly at her, his eyes glittering with an intense light as he tried to conceal his excitement. 'So… Are we saying…? Does this mean that er…sooner or later Manon would have left me regardless of how much of an insensitive *voyou* I am?'

Shari could hardly restrain a grin. He looked so chuffed to be off the hook.

'I dare say. Although she deserves a medal for how long she hung in there with all this ghastly yellow.'

He gave her a playful punch. 'She wanted it.'

She smiled. 'Yeah?'

Maybe she did. And maybe she didn't.

CHAPTER FIFTEEN

THE wedding was a glorious affair. There might have been Parisian couples in the past who'd outshone the Valentins, but most of those had been royal.

The ceremony in the *mairie*'s office was purely a bureaucratic formality, though the room had been decked with pink and white roses and a red carpet laid for the bride and groom. The real ceremony came afterwards, at the Eglise St-Eustache, a sixteenth century church with exquisitely stained glass.

The service itself was austere and beautiful.

Shari had forgotten Luc's connections in the air industry, or she wouldn't have been so surprised to discover that a friend of Luc's had volunteered his private jet to transport Neil and Emi, their children and two nannies to Paris for the festivities.

As it was, Shari was overjoyed.

Strangely, Neil and Emi were not as totally astounded by her and Luc's falling in love as Shari might have expected, though their approaching parenthood had come as a surprise.

As well, an elderly gentleman from Venice made the journey. When he'd first strolled into the *mairie's* and sat down beside his wife, Shari glimpsed a sudden rare shimmer in Luc's eyes.

A magnificent reception was held at the Ritz, one of the Hotel's last great events before it shut up shop for renovation. Everyone Shari and Luc knew in Paris was there, including some friends Shari had made at her language class.

Even if Neil hadn't been able to come, even if Shari hadn't been wearing a Valentino original, cut specifically to reveal the blue bird of happiness on her shoulder, just seeing her lover's joy would have made the day fantastic. As it was, it was sheerest heaven.

After the dancing, the toasts, the love and bonhomie of family and friends, Luc whisked his bride upstairs for one last splendid night in their favourite suite. Then in the morning, after a long and leisurely breakfast, he flew her to Italy for their honeymoon, where they planned to explore the Amalfi Coast for some weeks while their apartment was being renovated.

This time in palest ivory trimmed with softest aquamarine and a pale, pale, very watery blue, shades Shari knew suited her complexion perfectly.

It was a beautiful time of life.

EPILOGUE

'HERE,' Luc said. 'Give him to me. We don't want him to catch a chill.'

They were strolling together in the Rue Montorgueil. It was late in the day, and Shari felt the sudden cool snap in the breeze.

Although their baby boy was dressed well, the air could turn frosty in a second. Luckily Luc was wearing his padded jacket.

Shari handed the precious bundle over and Luc positioned him carefully inside his coat while Shari drew up the zipper.

'Not too far, now,' his father warned. 'Let him see out.'

Shari laughed as Luc-Henri chortled and his eyes, brown now and growing darker by the day, opened wide at the sudden change in his circumstances.

'There, now, isn't it lovely being held in Papa's arms? I quite like it myself.' Luc laughed with her, then she noticed him glance up at a passer-by and wave, his face alight with pride and pleasure.

Shari looked at the stranger. 'Who's that? Do I know him from somewhere?'

'Remember? He's the *boulanger* from the bakery near the fruit market.'

'Oh, of course. I know. How nice of him to wave. He must have noticed that ours is the most beautiful babe in Paris.'

'*And* he has the most beautiful *maman*.'

She smiled and planted a kiss on his bristly jaw. 'Thank you. That reminds me. Have you ever read *The Outlaw Earl?*'

He lifted his brows. 'I don't believe so. What happens in it?'

'Well, this beautiful lonely maiden is kidnapped from the home of her greedy parents by a wicked, but really hot earl.'

'Ah. And then what?' His eyes gleamed with a piercingly sensual light. 'Tell me.'

* * * * *

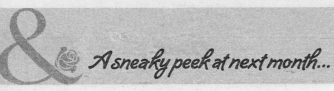

A sneaky peek at next month...

MODERN™

INTERNATIONAL AFFAIRS, SEDUCTION & PASSION GUARANTEED

My wish list for next month's titles...

In stores from 18th January 2013:

❑ Sold to the Enemy – Sarah Morgan

❑ Bartering Her Innocence – Trish Morey

❑ In the Heat of the Spotlight – Kate Hewitt

❑ Pride After Her Fall – Lucy Ellis

In stores from 1st February 2013:

❑ Uncovering the Silveri Secret – Melanie Milburne

❑ Dealing Her Final Card – Jennie Lucas

❑ No More Sweet Surrender – Caitlin Crews

❑ Living the Charade – Michelle Conder

❑ The Downfall of a Good Girl – Kimberly Lang

Available at WHSmith, Tesco, Asda, Eason, Amazon and Apple

Just can't wait?

Visit us Online

You can buy our books online a month before they hit the shops! **www.millsandboon.co.uk**

0113/01

Book of the Month

MILLS & BOON

Medical Romance

SCARLET WILSON
An Inescapable
Temptation

We love this book because...

Nurse Francesca Cruz takes a job on a cruise ship bound for the Mediterranean and finds herself trapped with gorgeous, arrogant doctor Gabriel Russo! Unable to escape temptation, the tension between these two reaches fever pitch and will have you longing for a cooling dip in the ocean!

On sale 1st February

Visit us Online

Find out more at
www.millsandboon.co.uk/BOTM

0113/BOTM

Special Offers

Every month we put together collections and longer reads written by your favourite authors.

Here are some of next month's highlights— and don't miss our fabulous discount online!

On sale 18th January

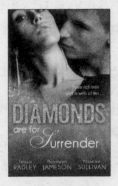

On sale 1st February

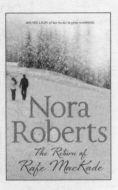

On sale 1st February

Save 20%
on all Special Releases

Find out more at
www.millsandboon.co.uk/specialreleases

Visit us
Online

0213/ST/MB399

 *2 Free Books!*

Join the Mills & Boon Book Club

Want to read more **Modern**™ books? We're offering you **2 more** absolutely **FREE!**

We'll also treat you to these fabulous extras:

- **Books up to 2 months ahead of shops**
- **FREE home delivery**
- **Bonus books with our special rewards scheme**
- **Exclusive offers and much more!**

Get your free books now!

Visit us Online

Find out more at **www.millsandboon.co.uk/freebookoffer**

SUBS/ONLINE/M

Mills & Boon® Online

Discover more romance at
www.millsandboon.co.uk

- 🌹 **FREE** online reads
- 🌹 **Books** up to one month before shops
- 🌹 **Browse our books** before you buy

...and much more!

For exclusive competitions and instant updates:

 Like us on **facebook.com/romancehq**

 Follow us on **twitter.com/millsandboonuk**

 Join us on **community.millsandboon.co.uk**

 Visit us Online Sign up for our FREE eNewsletter at **www.millsandboon.co.uk**

WEB/M&B/RTL4

The World of Mills & Boon®

There's a Mills & Boon® series that's perfect for you. We publish ten series and, with new titles every month, you never have to wait long for your favourite to come along.

Blaze®
Scorching hot, sexy reads
4 new stories every month

By Request
Relive the romance with the best of the best
9 new stories every month

Cherish™
Romance to melt the heart every time
12 new stories every month

Desire™
Passionate and dramatic love stories
8 new stories every month

Visit us Online

Try something new with our Book Club offer
www.millsandboon.co.uk/freebookoffer

M&B/WORLD2

What will you treat yourself to next?

*Ignite your imagination,
step into the past...*
6 new stories every month

INTRIGUE...

Breathtaking romantic suspense
Up to 8 new stories every month

*Captivating medical drama –
with heart*
6 new stories every month

MODERN™

*International affairs,
seduction & passion guaranteed*
9 new stories every month

n o c t u r n e™

*Deliciously wicked
paranormal romance*
Up to 4 new stories every month

RIVA™

*Live life to the full –
give in to temptation*
3 new stories every month available
exclusively via our Book Club

You can also buy Mills & Boon eBooks at
www.millsandboon.co.uk

*Visit us
Online*

M&B/WORLD2